John Culpepper the Merchant

Lori Crane

Copyright 2015 Lori Crane Entertainment
All rights reserved, including the right to reproduce this book
or any portion thereof in any form whatsoever.
For information, please email LoriCraneAuthor@gmail.com.

Published by Lori Crane Entertainment
Cover design: Robert Hess
Editor: Elyse Dinh-McCrillis at The Edit Ninja

www.LoriCrane.com

This book is a work of historical fiction.
Some names, characters, places, and incidents are from historical accounts.
Some names, characters, places, and incidents are products of the author's imagination.

ISBN: 978-0-9903120-7-9
ebook ISBN: 978-0-9903120-8-6

Family Lineage/Cast of Characters

John Culpepper the Merchant 1606-
John's wife: Mary Culpepper
Children: Henry Culpepper 1633-
Dennis "Denny" Culpepper 1637-
James Culpepper 1639-
Robert "Robbie" Culpepper 1641-
John "Johnny" Culpepper, Jr. 1644-

John's brother: Thomas Culpepper 1602-
Thomas's wife: Katherine St. Leger 1602-
Children: Anna Culpepper 1630-
Alex Culpepper 1632-
John "JJ" Culpepper 1633-
Frances Culpepper 1634-

John's uncle: Sir Alexander Culpepper 1570-1645
John's cousin: Lord John "JC" Culpepper, Baron of Thoresway 1599-
King Charles 1600-1649
Sir George Goring, Earl of Norwich 1585-
Oliver Cromwell 1599-
General Thomas Fairfax 1612-
Sir Edmund Plowden 1590-
Sir William Berkeley, Governor of Virginia 1605-

TABLE OF CONTENTS

January 4, 1642, London, England	9
October 1642, Jamestown, Virginia	15
November 1642, The Doldrums	25
December 1642, Greenway Court, Kent	29
January 1643, Oliver Cromwell	37
May 1643, To Virginia	45
June 1643, Chesapeake Bay	49
July 1643, Accomac, Virginia	65
January 1644, Greenway Court	73
1644, Boys	81
May 1645, Sir Alexander Culpepper	89
July 1645, Battle at Bridgewater	95
July 28, 1645, Accomac	103
October 1645, All Saints Church	113
September 1646, Henry Pedenden	121
June 3, 1647, Kidnap	129
November 11, 1647, Escape	131
December 26, 1647, Secret Treaty	135
June 1648, Battle at Maidstone	141
July 1648, Siege of Colchester	149
September 1648, Refuge at Leeds Castle	155
November 1648, Negotiations	159
January 20, 1649, Trial	167
January 30, 1649, Execution	175
February 5, 1649, Scotland's Proclamation	179
March 1649, Greenway Court	183
August 1649, The Thomas and John	189
Leeds Castle	195
To the Ship	197
To Virginia	205

Author's Notes	211
References	215
Books by Lori Crane	217
About the Author	219
Excerpt from *John Culpepper, Esquire*	221

CHAPTER 1

January 4, 1642, London, England

The king marched into the room unannounced. He walked through the middle of the active session of Parliament and was greeted with stunned silence. Never before had a monarch entered the House of Commons uninvited, and the nearly two hundred members present froze in place as if someone had painted their portrait, capturing the moment complete with paper strewn across tables, pens held in the air, and faces turned to pose for the painter. The king did not return their shocked gazes.

From his seat at a table in the center of the room, JC watched the king walk past him, easily slipping between the unmoving members of the House. JC's jaw fell open when the king sat in the speaker's chair. JC looked back toward the door, wondering how the king had entered the room without warning and saw the king's sergeant at arms blocking the doorway. Behind the intimidating man stood the king's soldiers — hundreds of them as far as JC could tell.

After a lengthy and excruciating silence, the king rose from the chair. The knuckles of his right hand turned white as he gripped the ball on top of his walking stick. His left hand remained at his side, balled into a fist.

"Gentlemen!" The king narrowed his eyes as he scrutinized each face. It was obvious he was not going to stay as he had neglected to remove his wide-brimmed hat, which matched his black velvet cloak. Underneath, he wore a red doublet and breeches, almost the same shade as his face. "I am sorry to have this occasion to come unto you, and I apologize for violating your parliamentary privilege." His beard twitched as he clenched his teeth. "But those guilty of treason have no privilege."

There was a collective gasp from the room, and a trickle of sweat dripped down JC's back. Parliament had not been convened for nearly nine years, as the king thought it his royal prerogative to rule the country alone, but after Scotland had invaded the north in retaliation for the king's religious rulings, he desperately needed money to fund his army. The only body that could legally raise taxes to fund an army was Parliament, so the king was forced to call on it. It denied the king's request to raise taxes, and instead compiled a list of over two hundred grievances against the king, demanding he address them. The document had been delivered a month ago but Parliament had never received word as to the king's reaction.

JC had not participated in the writing of the grievances. For the last nineteen years, he had worked in the king's service, just as his family had done for many kings and many generations. He would never contribute to anything as treasonous as telling the king how to rule. During his service, JC had never seen the king's demeanor this threatening. This unannounced visit to the House of Commons was not going to end well for someone.

The king lifted his hand and gestured for his sergeant at arms to enter the room.

All heads turned toward the door, and all eyes followed the sergeant as he walked to the middle of the room and unrolled a piece of paper. He held it with both hands in front of his face and turned clockwise as he read aloud. "I am commanded by His Majesty, my master, upon my allegiance that I should come to the House of Commons and request from Mr. Speaker five members of the House of Commons. When these gentlemen are delivered, I am commanded to arrest them in His Majesty's name for high treason. Their names are Mr.

Denzil Hollis, Sir Arthur Haselrig, Mr. John Pym, Mr. William Strode, and Mr. John Hampden."

The sergeant rolled up the paper and stuffed it back into his breast pocket.

JC witnessed a scowl cross the king's face while the sergeant read the names. The five men were the authors of the list of grievances.

"Mr. William Lenthall," the king bellowed.

A man wearing a black cape with a white collar emerged from the crowd and knelt before the king. "Yes, Your Majesty."

"Mr. Speaker, where are these men we seek? Do you see them in this room?"

Lenthall kept his eyes to the floor. "May it please Your Majesty, I have neither eyes to see nor tongue to speak in this place but only as the House is pleased to direct me, whose servant I am."

The king stared at the top of Lenthall's head. Lenthall remained still. No man risked a glance toward another or even dared to breathe for fear of attracting the king's attention. The king sighed and said, "I see all the birds have flown."

With a flick of his wrist, the king flipped his long hair off his shoulder and marched past Lenthall, leaving him kneeling in front of his own empty chair. The sergeant at arms followed the king from the room. When the door slammed, everyone exhaled.

CHAPTER 2

October 1642, Jamestown, Virginia Colony

It had been an unusually dry and warm fall. John Culpepper lay back on the wood slats, turning his face up to the sky, allowing the sun to wash over him and ease his tension. His dark curls fell back from his cheeks and a sigh of contentment escaped his lips. He could be sailing back to London very soon, perhaps tomorrow, and he was excited to see his wife and children. He had been in Jamestown for the last ten months, far longer than he had ever stayed before, but he felt he needed to remain in town until the Virginia General Assembly made its decision.

He was certain he already knew what

their final ruling would be. Who wouldn't want to make more money when possible? Of course the tax would pass. The council had been debating a six-pence-per-passenger tax on incoming ships, not only for newly arriving settlers, but also for members of the crews who sailed the ships, even though those men would be returning to sea as soon as the ship's provisions were secured. In the case of John's ship, the *Thomas and John,* which did not ferry passengers who could shoulder the new expense, the tax for his crew would come directly out of his profits. He stretched out on the bench outside the meetinghouse, crossed one boot over the other, and awaited word.

After an hour, one of the members of the council emerged from the building. "They passed the tax, John."

John sat up and frowned. "I guess I won't be docking in Jamestown anymore, then. I'll have to find another port for my ship."

He rose from the bench, waved goodbye to the man in the doorway, and headed to the wharf to share the disappointing news with his first mate, Benjamin. He stared down at the dusty ground as he walked, his worn, leather boots kicking up small clouds of dust since there hadn't been any significant rain in weeks. The towering pine trees that lined the road shaded him from the late afternoon sun. The bird's joyous songs were in stark contrast to his mood which had plunged with the news. He would have to stay longer. It would be months before he could return to England. How could the Jamestown assembly expect merchants to pay such a tax? The members were simply being greedy. After the last decade of begging and pleading for settlers to take root in the town, now they were going to charge them a tax for the pleasure of arriving. Most ship captains would complain about the tax but pay it regardless. John wasn't most captains, and he would do neither. He hadn't attended law school for four years without learning there was a way around every law and every tax, but it would be a time-consuming quest that would keep him in Virginia, searching for a new place to dock his ship.

As he walked, a breeze blew his dark curls off his forehead and tangled them around his collar. With each step, he calculated how long it would take to find a new dock. If he used his small boat to sail up the coast, he could probably find a place within a few weeks. Building a wooden pier would be a most laborious task, undoubtedly taking months to complete. One doesn't just pull an eighty-foot ship up to a sandy shore and tie it to a tree. And anchoring in the harbor while ferrying goods back and forth in smaller boats would be time-consuming and was not an option. The assembly's decision aggravated him to no end.

He was weary of being in Virginia. He was losing money by not sailing. More than anything, he longed to get back to the sea. She was his first love. Her white froth, deep swells, and endless horizons filled his soul like nothing else did. Finding a new port would keep him on land for at least another six months.

He ached to get home to Mary and his boys. Henry, the eldest of his four boys, would be nine this week. How did their birthdays keep slipping by without John's presence? The last time he was home, Mary mentioned that Denny and James kept questioning their father's whereabouts. She said she repeatedly explained to them that their father was working and would be home soon. Luckily, one-year-old Robbie was still too young to notice John's absence.

John smiled as he thought of his youngest. The curly-headed tyke was growing so fast, and John had seen him only once when he was two weeks old. Mary was upset with John for missing the birth, but one can't schedule stormy seas or predict early-born babies. He wondered if the boys were beginning to resent the fact he was never home, just like he'd resented his own father for the same reason.

His father, the bold and brazen Johannes Culpepper, wasn't a ship merchant. He was a lawyer, a large man with a temper to match. He ran his business from London, which was four hours from the first family home, the one they had left when John was five years old. Johannes stayed away for weeks at a time in those days. The second home was over a week's ride away from Johannes's office, and from the second home, his absence stretched into months. The lack of his father's presence was profoundly noticeable to John, leaving a deep scar of resentment in his heart that had lasted the entire thirty-six years of his life.

John shook his head in an attempt to erase the frustrating thoughts. Throughout his life, John had set his intention on becoming nothing like his father. Granted, John was gone for great lengths of time, but at least when John returned home, he remained home for six or eight weeks, sometimes twelve, and spent a lot of time with his growing sons, frequently carting them down to the dock to play on the ship while he loaded provisions for the next voyage. They loved the ship, and he loved to see their excited faces. Someday they would be old enough to sail with him. John looked forward to that day. Spending months at a time in the close confines of the ship would be the perfect opportunity to get to know his sons in a way he hadn't had the chance to thus far.

The smell of fish, rotting wood, and tar filled his nostrils as he neared the dock. He looked down the path that would momentarily open up into a bustling dockyard, and he wondered if he would ever be able to get Mary on his ship. He doubted it. She always had some excuse to not board the ship. She worried about weather and illness, though she always professed her husband to be a most talented and skillful captain.

"Mr. Culpepper, a letter arrived for you from London," the harbormaster called to him as he emerged into the clearing.

John picked up his pace, trotted over to the man, and thanked him. He looked down at the paper, smiling in anticipation of word from his wife. As he walked to the edge of the water, he turned the letter over and over. His name was written on the front and the red wax stamp of Wigsell Manor, his late grandfather's home, sealed the back. Mary wasn't in possession of such a stamp.

He sat down on a wooden crate, carefully snapped the seal, and unfolded the stiff paper. It was from his cousin JC. John's curiosity peaked as he had never before received a letter from JC.

JC was a knight in the service of the king, and John wondered what could be so important that JC would take time away from his demanding schedule to send a letter. For as long as John could remember, he had always admired his older cousin and knew him to be a most important man at court. The letter read:

My dear cousin,

It is with great foreboding that I write to you in light of our current events. As the members of Parliament had been summoned by His Majesty for the first time in quite some time, we were all rather excited to get on with the country's business at hand, but a few members took it upon themselves to design a document for the king. It contained over two hundred grievances toward His Majesty. I held my breath when it was delivered to the king in December, but the king remained silent about it for over a month. I had hoped he would ignore it, but I'm afraid he hasn't. In January, he unceremoniously barged into the House of Commons and attempted to arrest the five members responsible for penning the document. He didn't find them, as they had been forewarned and fled.

The following day, the bishops of the Church of England were turned away from the House of Lords meeting. Parliament had passed an act stating that the bishops could no longer attend those meetings. As you can imagine, the king was livid. He had not given his royal assent to such a scandalous act, so it was illegal when they enacted it. Even though the House of Lords knew this, they turned the bishops away. The bishops demanded the king do something about this Parliament run amok, but after the king's debacle at the House of Commons, he wasn't sure what could be done. It was becoming more and more apparent that Parliament was intentionally usurping the king's authority, and the king, not wanting to battle his own people, made haste to leave London at once, hoping Parliament's angst would die down in his absence.

I accompanied His Majesty with an army of two thousand men and we traveled north toward Nottingham Castle. While passing through Birmingham, we were ambushed, and the riotous crowd stole the king's silver plate and most of his household goods. There was nothing we could do to stop them. They held us at gunpoint. I will tell you now, the king was frightened for his life during that raid and has declared vengeance against those who participated. I have since learned they took his belongings to Warwick Castle, which they have declared a parliamentary stronghold.

Under great constraint, the king maintained his silence, but in June, Parliament sent a list of nineteen demands for the king to agree to if he is to avoid war and maintain his rightful place on the throne. They claimed control over the navy and the church, and demanded right-of-approval on the king's appointments. I'm afraid Parliament left him no choice. In August, he raised his standard at Nottingham, officially declaring war against Parliament. We've defeated them in a couple skirmishes at Southam and Powick Bridge, but we learned that they have taken over the king's royal army in London. They've amassed quite a militia and have strong support throughout the country. With the Scots holding Newcastle in the north and Parliament holding London in the south, it seems we sit between two capable armies.

I'm sorry to be the bearer of this bad news, cousin, but our country and our kin are now at war, brother against brother, countrymen against countrymen. After seeing to the king's safety at Nottingham, I have taken Queen Henrietta Maria and Princess Mary from England for safekeeping, and I and our ally, George Goring, are attempting to garner support from our neighboring countries. I will not divulge in this correspondence my whereabouts as it would be unsafe for the royal family.

You must sail home immediately to see to the wellbeing of your wife and children. Your brother and your uncle have joined with others in attempts of raising an army in Kent. They will need your help. Please make haste in your journey.

Your cousin,
JC

Parliament had been at odds with the king since his coronation in 1625, but did it really see war as the only option? John reread the letter three times before he jumped up from the crate. He hurried across the wharf toward his ship, his mind racing. Suddenly, Virginia's new passenger tax and searching for a new place to dock his ship didn't seem so important after all. He needed to return to England—now.

Thunderheads loomed on the horizon behind his ship, and the first winds of a coming storm whipped at his face. He approached the vessel, yelling for his first mate.

"Benjamin! Benjamin, where are you?"

Benjamin stuck his head over the railing of the great ship, his scraggly hair falling over his weathered face, almost hiding the fact he had very few teeth left. "I'm here, sir. What was the outcome at the general assembly?"

"Never mind that now. Prepare to make sail. Our country has gone to war."

"Virginia? With the Indians?"

"No, England with the king. We leave at dawn."

Unshaken by the news, Benjamin thumbed over his shoulder at the advancing storm clouds. "We won't have good weather tomorrow, Cap'n, and we don't have a full crew."

"Well, then, get a full crew. We'll sail the day after. Make it happen. My family's lives may depend upon it."

"Aye, Cap'n."

CHAPTER 3

November 1642, The Doldrums

The *Thomas and John* sat idle, unmoving in the dim morning light. Her sails hung limp, as they had for the last two days. John ran his hands through his hair and impatiently tapped his foot as he stared across her bow at the unending sea of glass before him. The water blended with the sky, creating a mist as far as the eye could see. There was no horizon, just an endless mirror of foggy steel blue.

He never thought this place existed and had never experienced it on any of his prior journeys, but now, when he most needed to make haste, he found his ship stuck in the middle of it. They called it the doldrums—the place in the ocean where no wind billowed sails, no waves lapped against hulls, and no mighty vessels leapt across the breakers. John had heard tales of ships being stuck in the doldrums for weeks at a time. He prayed this wouldn't be the case, but on this third morning, he was beginning to wonder if they'd ever break free of it. He'd heard ancient legends of ships carrying horses beneath their decks, and when they found themselves stuck in the doldrums, the crew would build cranes, lower the horses into the water, and allow them to pull the ship. He didn't know if those stories were true, for he had never witnessed a horse swimming, but in any case, he wasn't carrying any horses. He was, however, carrying two small rowboats.

"Drop the boats!" he yelled to Benjamin. "We'll row."

"Sir?" Benjamin approached. "You want the crew to row us out of the doldrums?"

"Yes, Benjamin. Put them to oar. See to it at once."

"Yes, sir."

* * *

The men dropped the small boats into the water, tied them to the ship, and began to row. They struggled against the weight of their load, but ever so slowly, the majestic ship began to creep forward.

"How long do you think we'll have to row?" one of the sailors asked another next to him.

"Until the cap'n gets her back to wind...or until we're all dead. Whichever comes first."

"Stop talking and keep rowing!" Benjamin bellowed from the bow.

For the next thirty hours, the sailors took turns rowing. The only movement in the water surrounding them came from the small ripples caused by their oars. After more than a day, the limp sails picked up a small draft and began swaying in the midafternoon sun.

"Sir!" yelled a sailor from one of the boats.

Benjamin turned and saw the sailor pointing up toward the sails. He looked up and saw the sails flutter in the breeze, and an uncommon grin spread across his unshaven face. He jogged to the back of the ship and descended the creaking, wooden steps to the lower deck. He dropped his head below the opening and blinked to adjust to the dim light. "Cap'n, she's back to wind!"

"Finally!" John jumped from behind his scarred, wooden desk and followed Benjamin up the steps. On deck, he raised his hand to block the sun's rays as he looked up at the fluttering sails. A cold, Atlantic breeze blew across John's face, the first he had felt in four days, and he laughed out loud. "Ha! We've cleared the doldrums! Benjamin, hoist the sails and get us underway."

"Aye, sir. Hoist the sails!"

Almost instantly, there was a flurry of activity on the upper deck as weathered sailors began pulling up the small boats, climbing the masts, raising the sails, and shouting commands.

"We have a lot of time to make up," John said. "I want to be in London within the week."

"Aye, sir!"

CHAPTER 4

December 1642, Greenway Court, Kent

On a cold, foggy evening, the crew secured the *Thomas and John* to the wooden dock at Blackwall on the Thames. John jumped from the ship onto the dock, not waiting for the crew to set the gangway into place. He then ran to the livery, hired an old mare, and rode to Greenway Court. The manor house was a four-hour ride south from London and had been in his family for generations. He had lived there as a child, but his older brother, Thomas, was the one who inherited it. Mary and the boys had been living with Thomas's family for the last eight years while John sailed to and from Virginia, and for that, John was eternally grateful.

He arrived at the house as the first stars appeared in the eastern horizon, excited to see its dark silhouette against the purple sky, and even more eager to see his wife. He jumped down from the old mare while it was still walking and burst through the front door, calling, "Mary! Mary!"

A servant girl peeked out from the dining room door on his right and another from the reception room on his left. Thomas appeared at the top of the stairs.

"Brother, you would never make a living as a thief." Thomas bounced down the stairs with a smile and hugged his younger brother.

"Thomas, I came as soon as I heard about the king. Are Mary and the children all right?"

"Yes, they're fine. We're all fine. Did you just arrive in London?" Thomas gestured for the girl in the reception room to come take John's hat and cloak.

John nodded. "I've never ridden so fast in my life. I probably nearly killed that old mare I was riding." He handed his things to the girl.

"John?" a soft whisper came from the top of the stairs.

She appeared like a spirit in the soft, flickering candlelight that illuminated the staircase, and she floated down the steps in her nightdress and robe. The light in the entryway glowed on her ivory complexion, and John thought she looked like an angel descending from the heavens.

"Mary!" John met his wife at the bottom step and wrapped his arms around her. The servants disappeared around the corners as he kissed her tenderly, entwining his fingers in her long brown hair. "I've missed you so."

"And I've missed you, husband. I'm so happy

you're home."

"Well, I'll give you two some privacy." Thomas squeezed past them and ascended the stairs.

Thomas's wife, Katherine, appeared at the top of the stairs. "John, is that you?"

"Yes. Hello, Katherine."

"Oh, John, we're so glad you've returned." She descended the stairs, touched her husband's arm as she passed him. She came all the way down the stairs and hugged John. "Did Thomas tell you about the king? Our country is in such a terrible state." She couldn't stop the tears from falling.

"I heard, dear sister. That is why I've returned, to see to your safety." He released Katherine and looked down at Mary. "Where are my boys?"

"I just put them to bed. You'll have to see them in the morning." She took his hand. "Come into the kitchen and let me get you something to drink and eat." Mary pulled him into the dining room, calling for the kitchen girl to stoke the fire to warm some food.

John followed his wife and heard his brother and sister-in-law ascend the creaking staircase. He would speak with Thomas about the state of the country tomorrow. First, he wanted to spend time with his wife.

A servant boy lit the massive fireplace in the dining room while the kitchen girl brought John a plate of food and poured him a cup of cider. Mary and John sat at the table in the opulent room, holding hands and talking about the boys, the country, the king, and the new tax passed in Virginia until the wee hours of the morning. As the first golden light of morning entered the room through the east windows, John's boys descended the stairs in a stampede and were surprised to find their father sitting at the table. As soon as Thomas, Katherine, and their four children joined them, breakfast was served, and as exhausted as John was, he was elated to be home with his family. He felt immense relief that the war had not reached his family home.

The table was lively and animated as eight children all talked to John at the same time as if vying for his attention.

"Father, we had a colt born just yesterday," said Henry.

"He's brown with four white socks just like your horse, Gabby. Do you want to go out and see him?" asked Denny.

"I'll go out a little bit later, Denny," replied John.

Before he even finished his sentence, James piped in as well. "And we went into London just last week. Are you going to go into London while you're here, Father?"

John nodded. "Yes, I'll probably take a trip into town. Would you like to go with me?"

James nodded eagerly while taking a drink of his milk, causing some of it to dribble down his chin. Mary reached over and wiped the boy's face with a napkin.

"Did Mother tell you about the soldiers we saw marching across our land?" Henry asked.

Their eight-year-old cousin Alex joined in. "Father said they were Parliament's soldiers. Have you ever seen them before, Uncle John?"

John shook his head and opened his mouth to ask his brother what Parliament's soldiers were doing on Culpepper land, but the boys wouldn't allow him to get a word in edgewise.

His brother shrugged as the din of chatter and silver tapping against china kept him from commenting, also.

John listened to the children with great attention, amazed at how much they had grown in his absence. Henry had been but an infant when John first bought his ship. John suddenly remembered the birthday gift he had brought for his eldest son. He pulled a small, intricately carved wooden Indian from his pocket and handed it to Henry.

"Thank you, Father!" Henry ran around the table and hugged his father. "Does this look like a real Indian?"

Denny and James jumped up from their chairs to look at the small statue.

"Yes, with the feathered headdress and all."

Mary picked up Robbie, held him on her lap, and bounced him up and down. "If you're all finished eating, why don't you and your cousins run upstairs and get dressed?" Mary said.

Five boys and two girls ran from the room and pounded up the stairs, yelling and laughing.

"I'll see to them," Katherine said, rising from the table. She took Robbie from Mary's arms.

Thomas rose and followed his wife from the room, leaving Mary and John alone once again.

Mary smiled at her husband. "I'm so glad you're home, John. The boys missed you. We've all missed you."

John sipped his warm cider and looked at his wife over the rim of his cup. He placed it down on the table. "I'm glad to be home, too."

"Did Thomas write to you about the king?" she asked.

"No, JC did. It sounds as if the king has found himself in quite a predicament."

She nodded. "Did JC tell you about the Catholic prayer book?" Without awaiting his response, she continued, "The king demanded the Scots use it, and they retaliated by invading England and seizing Newcastle. I think that's what started this whole war."

"Well, that's probably one of the causes, my dear, but I'm sure that's not the only reason. The king is just doing what he thinks is best for his people."

The kitchen girl appeared behind him, took his plate, and poured more cider into his cup.

"Does he think Catholicism best for Scotland?" Mary asked.

"It seems he does."

"Does he think it best for England also?"

John shrugged. "We'll have to wait and see."

"What if he demands we use the prayer book here?" Her eyes were wide.

John sipped, swallowed, and shook his head. "I don't think he'll do that. We've been the Church of England for far too long to go back now, and the king is certainly not in any position to pass any proclamations right now. Nonetheless, you shouldn't worry yourself over such notions. JC and Thomas both have their ears to the throne. If anything were to happen, we'd be the first to know. Since JC is now the protector of the queen and Princess Mary, our family is very well vested at court. We will safeguard the royal family, and in turn, we will be well protected."

Mary's face turned dark. "John, there is no more court."

John had no argument or response. She was correct.

Almost six years earlier, the king had imposed Anglican services on the Scots, introducing the Book of Common Prayer and forcing the Scottish Presbyterian Church to conduct its services as the king directed. Scottish delegations had traveled to England numerous times wishing to discuss this religious intrusion and perhaps negotiate some sort of agreement, but they were sent home again and again, never allowed an audience with the king. The Scots, having no alternative, finally invaded England and seized Newcastle. Parliament, which was mostly Presbyterian and sympathetic to the Scots' cause, refused to fund an army to engage them as the king wished. The kind disbanded Parliament out of spite.

Mary had voiced feelings identical to those of most of England's citizens. The Scots were not the only ones distressed by the religious ruling. Citizens of England figured if the king could do something so inconceivable in Scotland, what was to stop him from doing the same thing in England? For the last few years, men had gathered in and around London behind closed doors to discuss what to do about the oppressive rulings of this dictator. These were a few of the smoldering embers of the war the king was now facing.

If this had been the only issue, it probably would have faded away with time. But in addition to demanding the Scots use the Catholic prayer book, the king had made numerous religious decisions the people of England found deeply troublesome. At the beginning of his rule and against Parliament's wishes, the king had married the Catholic princess Henrietta Maria, who Parliament was certain would turn the king's ear. Later, he allowed his army to attack the Presbyterians in Spain and France, and illegally raised taxes on his people to fund those battles.

One of the king's most disturbing decisions was placing a Catholic supporter in the position of archbishop of Canterbury. It was a catastrophic appointment followed by rebellions and revolts. But the king's most ruinous act of all was disbanding Parliament when it wouldn't support his war efforts. He ruled the country alone for nearly a decade. The word *tyranny* had crossed many lips, and the words *uprising* and *war* had crossed many more.

The king finally called Parliament back into session when he needed to fund his war against the Presbyterian Scots, which Parliament refused to do. Instead, it presented him with the list of grievances, and he was now facing the repercussions of his past actions. The people of England had had enough.

CHAPTER 5

January 1643, Oliver Cromwell

A few weeks later, John and his brother rode through a cold and damp fog into London and went for an ale at the Blackwall Inn. They removed their hats and scarfs and took a seat at the dank, corner table nearest the soot-encrusted fireplace that was glowing warm with embers.

Thomas was four years older than John and the two had always been inseparable as children. In their teens, they attended law school together at their father's insistence, but Thomas was the only one who fulfilled their father's dreams of them practicing law. Thomas had been called to the bar and opened law chambers in London. Reluctantly, John joined him as a lawyer for a few years. Mary was the first to recognize how sullen and sad John was and insisted he give up his law practice to follow his childhood dream of owning a ship. John had asked Thomas for help with the financing, and within a few months, he purchased his ship. Immediately, John was a happier man, but his father never spoke to him again.

A scrawny boy placed a few logs into the fireplace, and the brothers watched the red embers grow into a roaring fire. They ordered a couple pints of ale, and once the barkeep delivered the mugs to the table, Thomas began to fill John in on all the unrest in the land that John had missed over the previous year.

"JC wrote me of the king trying to arrest those five members of the House of Commons and of his raising his standard at Nottingham, but what happened in between?" John asked.

Thomas took a drink and sighed. "Did he tell you about Cromwell?"

John shook his head.

"After the fiasco in the House of Commons, the king fled London and was ambushed in Birmingham."

"JC told me that."

"That attack was instigated by Oliver Cromwell."

"Who's Oliver Cromwell?"

"Exactly. He's a nobody, a man of modest means, barely inside the gentry class. He's sat in Parliament for a few years but has been pretty much useless and quiet. His only claim is that he led a single cavalry troop some years ago, and for some reason, Parliament thought that enough to elevate his status. They placed him in charge of their cavalry. He's a committed Puritan with deep-rooted desires to take the king down because of his past religious rulings. After remaining quiet and never participating in Parliament's dealings for years, somehow he convinced Parliament to pass what he called the Militia Ordinance, proclaiming the people of London are bound by law to join Parliament's militia if called, and he immediately began recruiting men of low birth."

"What's the punishment for not joining?"

"Beheading."

John exhaled and shook his head in disbelief.

Thomas continued. "He's not recruiting military men or men of gentry, he's recruiting anyone he can get his hands on. He's not a trained military leader, so from a strategic standpoint, it's difficult to guess his next move."

"How many men does he have now?"

"Probably twice as many as we do. He took over the king's royal army in London and is recruiting men by force."

"Have the members of Parliament lost their minds?"

"Apparently so, but not all of them. Many members have disappeared to their country homes. They refuse to participate in taking down the king. The ones who are left, like Cromwell, are now jockeying for position in what they think will be a new country. Parliament is supposed to represent the people, but sadly, the citizens are now afraid of Parliament and the king is nowhere to be found to protect them. Without an option, they're joining Cromwell's militia in droves."

John groaned and looked down into his mug.

An older woman with slivers of gray in her long red hair set two more pints on their table.

"Thank you," John said.

"You're Culpeppers," she said, unquestionably.

John nodded.

She looked into John's eyes. "You look just like your father."

"Excuse me, do I know you?" John asked.

"No, you don't know me." She smiled and pointed at the mugs. "These pints are on the house. Tell your father to come by and visit."

"Our father is long dead, madam," Thomas said.

She spun her head to look at Thomas, shock in her eyes. "Oh, I'm sorry. I didn't know." A flash of sadness crossed her face and she looked back at John.

John wondered how this lowly, tavern

wench knew a man of his father's importance. She was middle aged with soft wrinkles around her eyes, but he could tell by her prominent cheekbones and full lips that she had probably been quite beautiful in her younger days. Perhaps this wench was the reason his father remained in London for lengthy stretches of time so many years ago.

The woman's eyes became misty. "I'm very sorry to hear that. I was rather fond of your father. Well, if you ever need anything, my son owns the fishery in Maidstone, right on the River Medway. His name is Waller and the place is called Waller's. You tell him his mother sent you."

John and Thomas looked quizzically at each other and then Thomas said, "Um, Waller's. All right. Thank you for the information, madam."

"Of course." She nodded at Thomas and slowly backed up from the table, stealing fleeting glances at John. "Just like your father," she mumbled.

"Well, back to the king. The story gets worse," Thomas said as John tried unsuccessfully to ignore the strange woman's continual stares. "After the attack in Birmingham, the king went to Kingston upon Hull to secure his arsenal and found Cromwell's men guarding the town. They were refused entrance. JC and Uncle Alexander were at the king's side, and they retreated to Howorth Moor, outside of York, to gather as many men as they could summon and create a plan to force their way in. I joined them with three hundred of my own men, and we laid siege upon the town to retrieve the arsenal. What we didn't know was while we were gathering our men at Howorth Moor, Cromwell was recruiting an army inside the town to keep us at bay."

"What happened?"

"We couldn't break their defenses. Our invasion failed. What happened to the king—first being attacked and robbed in Birmingham, and then being turned away from his own weapon stores—told us all that we needed to know. It was blatantly evident that Parliament was making a bold, political move, a move that could lead to war. Perhaps that's what they wanted. We escorted the king up to Nottingham, and after Parliament delivered their demands that they knew the king would never agree to, he raised his standard and declared war. Parliament has garnered a massive amount of support and has taken over most of the royal army in the south. Now we find ourselves fighting our own countrymen, many of whom are family and friends."

John dropped his head and ran his fingers through his hair, his elbows on the table. "Well, perhaps only friends. Our family would never fight against the king."

"I'm sorry to tell you this, brother, but our cousin Nicholas as taken Parliament's side."

"Nicholas, the scholar?"

"Yes. I haven't seen him, but I heard through Uncle Alexander that Nicholas is no longer in the king's service."

"That's unbelievable. A Culpepper fighting the king? I hope you don't run into him at any battles."

"I don't think he's been involved in any thus far. Fortunately, all of the skirmishes have happened in the north. There's been no fighting south of London, so no one has seen Nicholas and our families have been safe."

"Thank almighty God. When I received JC's letter, I was terrified. I was so anxious to get home and horrified I wouldn't be able to find you once I arrived. I didn't know if you were still at Greenway Court or had placed the family in hiding or, God forbid, if you were all dead."

"You had every right to be frightened, brother. It was a confusing time and we didn't know what was going to happen when the king declared war. We didn't know how large Parliament's army actually was."

"Do you think our families will remain safe?" asked John.

"Yes, unless we lose. If Parliament's uprising is successful, we will all be in danger. Until then, our wives and children are safe." Thomas gulped the last of the ale and rose.

On their way out of the tavern, John glanced back and noticed the redheaded woman still staring at him. She smiled and waved goodbye. He reluctantly waved back.

CHAPTER 6

May 1643, To Virginia

John, Mary, and the boys sat at the table in the opulent dining room of Greenway Court with the morning sun shining through the windows. They were surrounded by dark oak-paneled walls, thick velvet curtains held back by gold ropes and tassels, and beautiful paintings of family members that had been on those walls for decades. Ornate silver candlestick holders graced the center of the table.

"I need to head back to Virginia," John said. "I've loved being home with you and the children, but after five months, I must get back to minding my business."

Mary placed her cup down and frowned.

"How long will you be gone this time?"

"It may be quite a while. I need to find a way around that new tax. Jamestown has been a convenient port for my business, but now it's simply become too expensive. Benjamin and I are going to search around Chesapeake Bay for a new place to dock. It doesn't make sense to pay tax on sailors who are only going to be in town for a few weeks to provision the ship. Once we find a new place to dock, we need to build a new warehouse and probably a pier to host the ship. That's going to take some time." John shoveled some eggs into his mouth.

Robbie waddled up to Mary and she picked him up. "How much time?" She rocked Robbie back and forth as he snuggled into her bosom and placed his thumb in his mouth.

"Probably five or six months at least." John watched Robbie on his mother's lap and thought it the most heartwarming sight he had ever witnessed. A wave of guilt washed over him and he wished he could remain home longer. "I shall miss you and the boys very much," he said.

"And we shall miss you, husband. You need to return home as soon as you can."

"You shouldn't worry, Mary. The war isn't coming this far south. Thomas will guard you well."

"I'm not worried about the war. I know you wouldn't leave us if you thought we were in any danger."

"No, Thomas assured me you're not in any danger." He looked across the table at his boys, who were devouring breakfast like they would never eat again. The sight made him smile for a moment. He turned his attention back to his own plate and scooped some eggs onto his fork. "If you're not worried about the war, why do you request that I return soon?"

"Because I gave birth to Robbie while you were away, and I don't want to have another child without you present."

John jerked his attention from his plate to his wife.

She smiled and nodded, her eyes twinkling. She glanced at the row of boys sitting at the table. "Perhaps I'll give you a daughter this time."

John laughed and gestured at his sons. "She'll probably starve."

Mary laughed, too. "Please return by Yuletide so you can greet your new child properly."

John placed his fork back on his plate and rose from the table. He bent over his wife and infant son, kissing Mary on the forehead and rubbing his hand across Robbie's hair. Robbie looked up at him with big blue eyes, tugging at John's heart. John looked into Mary's eyes. "You have my word, wife. I shall leave immediately and return in time for the birth."

John stood up straight and tugged at the bottom of his doublet. "Who wants to go to the dock with me and help me provision the ship?" he said to his boys.

The three older boys yelled and jumped up from the table at the same time. Robbie stirred in his mother's arms but quickly snuggled back into her warmth the moment the older boys were gone. He placed his thumb back in his mouth and fell asleep.

"Don't forget your coats," Mary called after her sons, not that they heard her.

"We'll give you a little peace and quiet today. I'll have them home in time for supper."

CHAPTER 7

June 1643, Chesapeake Bay

"Land ho!" Benjamin yelled, looking through the brass telescope.

"Let me see," said John, strutting across the deck and reaching for the telescope.

He saw the green horizon of a tree line before them. Coming into Virginia always made him smile. More and more it felt like home to him, even though his family was an ocean away. "Take her into the bay, Benjamin."

"Yes, Cap'n."

Riding the crest of the cobalt waves, the ship entered Cape Charles Harbor with Port Comfort sitting on her starboard side. After a while, the James River appeared on her port side. That was where they would usually sail into to dock at Jamestown, but today they would continue north into Chesapeake Bay. A multitude of seabirds circled the ship, cawing and whistling their welcome. John hadn't seen birds since they left London six weeks earlier. He looked up through the spiderweb of hemp ropes and the white billowing sails and watched them for a long time, thanking God for a safe arrival and an uneventful journey. They had run into no storms, no bad weather, and most of all, no doldrums. Even though he had a busy few months ahead of him searching for a new place to dock, the familiar Virginia shoreline made John's heart swell with happiness.

The ship entered the Chesapeake Bay with the mainland of Virginia to her left and a peninsula to her right. John had decided the peninsula would be the place to explore for a new place to dock. Eventually, the port tax would spread up the coast of Virginia, and John didn't want to tackle this project again in a few years.

As the ship navigated north through the bay, they scouted the shoreline of the peninsula and eventually saw the mouth of a river. There, a few larger ships were anchored in the bay. John knew they were too large to navigate the river, but if they were anchored there, something must be up river. John's boat, being a shallow draught, would have no problem navigating the waterway.

He told Benjamin to take her into the river, and after a while, they came upon a small dock. It was nothing more than a few small boats tied up next to a worn and rickety pier, but it had possibilities. The wharf wasn't the settled waterfront John was used to docking at in Jamestown, and it certainly wasn't the bustling dock he had left on the Thames, but there would be no taxes this far up in the bay.

John scanned the land and saw nothing on the shore except one shack and a few wagons and horses. A half dozen young boys emerged from the tree line, running toward the water, waving and yelling at the ship, obviously offering to help her dock. Well, at least John and his crew were being welcomed by more than seabirds, and if there were children here, there had to be adults nearby.

The crew dropped the rowboats to help guide the massive ship. They turned her and slowly piloted her toward the land, with the dirty-faced boys assisting in bringing her ashore. Ropes flew through the warm summer air, men shouted directions, and after an hour of securing the ship to the decrepit pier, her gangway was finally set into place.

John was the first to disembark, strutting like a peacock down the walkway onto the first solid ground he had seen in six weeks. The lads, glistening with sweat, welcomed him to

Accomac, Virginia. John asked one of the boys if he knew who was in charge, and the lad pointed to the shack at the edge of the clearing, stating that's where John would find the dockmaster. John pulled coins from his pocket and offered them to the boys, who greedily grabbed them and ran off.

After John greeted the dockmaster and told him about his cargo, the old man pointed John in the direction of Nathaniel Littleton's house two miles up the road. He was told Mr. Littleton would instruct him on the unloading and storing of his cargo and supplying his ship with new provisions.

John walked up the narrow road, more of a cow path really, passing insignificant shacks, shops, and the occasional chicken pecking for morsels in the overgrown grasses on the side of the dusty road. The humid smell of moss and the sharp scent of pine trees encircled his head. He loved those smells. A small gray donkey munched on grass behind a picket fence and it stopped eating to bray at John as he passed. John covered his ears and laughed. He didn't realize donkeys were so loud. Wild flowers grew in the field behind the animal's enclosure. Accomac was quite a beautiful and pleasant place, reminding him of the land surrounding his grandfather's estate in Sussex where he spent summers as a boy.

John finally arrived at Mr. Littleton's

shack and knocked on the door. He was greeted by a barrel-shaped man who sported deep lines around his narrow blue eyes and a mustache speckled with gray. The man was holding a half-eaten chicken leg and grease glistened on his mustache.

"How may I help you, sir?" the man asked as he chewed.

"Greetings, Mr. Littleton. I was told to see you about unloading my ship. My name is John Culpepper, captain of the *Thomas and John*. We just docked in Accomac."

Littleton tossed the chicken leg across the yard and it was immediately gobbled up by a gristly hound dog who had been sleeping under the front porch. The man wiped his greasy hand on the chest of his shirt and reached out to shake John's hand. "Well, hello, Captain Culpepper. Always nice to have newcomers to our little community." The man grabbed his hat from the hook near the door and stepped out, leading John back down the road toward the dock. He placed his hat on his balding head as he walked. "How was your journey?"

"Delightfully uneventful, but we're happy to be back on solid ground. And please call me John."

"Very well, John. Tell me, what kind of cargo are you carrying?"

"We brought powder, shot, hatchets, cutlery wares, blankets, farming tools."

"That's wonderful. Lord knows we can use all those things. Shipments from England are far and few between around here. Most ships dock in Jamestown so we only get the leftover goods delivered here to Accomac."

"I used to dock in Jamestown, but if we could make arrangements, I'd like to dock here from now on. I need to move all my stores to a local warehouse if that's possible, then secure some local goods to resupply my ship and return to London."

"We can certainly arrange that. We'll soon harvest tobacco, and there's always timber you can take back with you. There's a large storehouse for rent not far from the dock."

"Do you think I could lease it for the time being?"

"Well, I'm the one who owns it so I would say yes."

John chuckled. "That's wonderful news."

"Are you carrying any settlers with you?" Littleton asked.

"No, sir, just goods."

"All right, then. We'll get you set up."

Accomac had a population of one thousand, as opposed to the fifteen thousand settlers scattered throughout the coast of the rest of Virginia, so there weren't as many amenities or workers available to help John build a new warehouse, but it made financial sense to invest in a dock and warehouse in Accomac and save on the imposed tax in Jamestown.

For the next few days, Benjamin and the sailors unloaded the ship while John traveled through the town, making commerce deals with the local residents. Within days, he made arrangements to return to London with timber and local sundries, and secured agreements to take back tobacco on the next trip following the harvest. John knew he'd get a good price for the timber, as everyone in London needed wood since most of the trees in England had been long felled. He also found a nice plot of land not far from the dock and purchased it. All John needed to do now was decide how long he would allow his ship to remain in Virginia. He could use his sailors' help building his new warehouse, but it would probably cost more to feed them than they were worth. Sometimes they were a lazy bunch, and even though they were good sailors, he wasn't sure if they knew anything about building.

John ordered timber for the construction of his warehouse, and opted to bring some local carpenters over from Jamestown. It was expensive to transport them to Accomac and feed them for the duration of the build, but at least the warehouse would be built correctly. He would send his ship back to London immediately and allow his sailors to do what they did best—sail.

Benjamin oversaw the loading of the ship

for the next week, and when the task was finished, John sent the ship back to London. He watched the crew pull her into the river and raise her white sails. They fluttered for a moment, then caught the breeze and snapped. He watched them billow as she slowly floated westward toward the Chesapeake. He felt a little queasy watching his ship leave him behind, but he trusted Benjamin. Benjamin was probably the *only* member of his boisterous crew he trusted. Benjamin knew how to offload the supplies and was more than capable of handling the crew. He was a dependable and reliable partner.

Once the ship sailed, John found himself feeling edgy about being stuck in Virginia. Given the political turmoil in his country and his wife's delicate condition, he was extremely anxious about being away for such a long time. But not only did he need to build a new warehouse, he also needed to build a house for himself. There were no inns in Accomac, so until he could put a roof over his head, he would be forced to sleep under the stars.

As the weeks passed, he thought of his family constantly and felt the usual guilt that he wasn't home to watch over them and witness his boys growing. Robbie would be nearly three by the time John stepped foot on English soil again. He looked across the building site, strewn with planks and logs and tools, and wondered what Mary would think of it. He wished she was here.

He closed his eyes and pictured her lovely face and warm smile. He couldn't wait to wrap his arms around her again. The sea was a beautiful mistress, but she did not keep him warm at night.

That night John lay under the stars looking straight up into the trees, watching the pinpoints twinkle through the leaves and the fireflies dance around him. He listened to the chirp of the crickets. His mind wandered back to his youth. Since he was a boy, he'd loved ships, and nearly every member of his family, especially his father, had scoffed at his idea of owning one. Well, his father didn't merely scoff. Many times he downright flew into a rage, screaming that he would disinherit and disown John if John bought a ship. But after less than a decade, John was making more money than any of them. The men in his family were lawyers, knights, barons, country gentlemen. They would never do anything as common as sail a ship. They certainly wouldn't be caught lying on the hard ground in Accomac, Virginia, counting the stars.

He listened to an owl hooting in the distance and watched the pine trees swaying above his head. John was different than the rest of the men in his family. He had always been different. He had no desire to sit around idle in the countryside and be a country gentleman. He had no desire to sit in an office and shuffle legal papers. At the age of fifteen, he'd been sent off to law school but he despised every minute of it. It was the last thing John wanted to do. The paperwork, the arguing, the rhetoric was enough to make him want to crawl in a hole and never come out again. The only members of his family who encouraged his dream of sailing were his wife and his brother. He wouldn't have bought a ship without Mary's blessing, and he couldn't have bought the ship if it weren't for Thomas's financial help. Thomas had paid for half the ship, and John named it the *Thomas and John*.

After nine years of voyages, John was convinced, even though it tore at his heart to be away from his family for long stretches of time, that he had made the right decision in giving up his law practice and becoming a merchant. Over the years, he had made good connections in Virginia and had set up warehouses in Jamestown and London and had filled them both to capacity. Soon he would have a new warehouse in Accomac. He never considered himself the good lawyer his father wanted him to be, but he was certainly a good merchant and an even better sailor. John's trips to Virginia made more money than anyone in his aristocratic family had ever thought possible, and Thomas was more than pleased with his share of the income the ship produced.

John thought about the tax imposed in

Jamestown. Perhaps all those years of studying law at Middle Temple was finally paying off for him—in finding ways to get around the laws. Hence his docking in Accomac. On top of the financial benefits this arrangement provided, he liked the small, fishing town. It was quaint, and the few residents he had met so far were very cordial. He had been warmly welcomed into the community.

The history of the *Thomas and John* hadn't all been pleasant and without event. Some days were fraught with terrible storms, other days some of John's men were forced to remain in Virginia or London due to illness. But the worst day was May 10, 1636, when his original first mate, Richard Lambert, died of scurvy on board. John would never forget that voyage. Lambert had been John's right hand. John was still new to sailing a ship, and he was quite sure he couldn't navigate her without Lambert. Every member of his crew was sick that journey, and there were endless days when John didn't know if they would ever reach their destination. He could have lost his entire crew and ended up floating aimlessly on the ocean until sun and starvation killed him.

Sadly but fortunately, Lambert's was the only life lost on that fateful voyage, and the second mate, Benjamin, proved to be an admirable first mate. Benjamin stepped into the role without hesitation, flawlessly navigated the ship on to Virginia, and had been John's best sailor and dearest friend for the last seven years.

John glanced around at his newly purchased land that was glowing in the light of the full moon. It was quite beautiful. He used two of the headrights in his possession to acquire the plot and sold a third to Nathaniel Littleton, which in turn financed the construction of his warehouse. He wondered what Thomas would say about collecting headrights now. Headrights were granted by the king to each traveler in an attempt to settle the new land. They were worth fifty to one hundred acres each. On previous voyages to Virginia, John had transported a few passengers in exchange for their headrights, but Thomas was not happy about the arrangement. For such a smart lawyer, it was strange that Thomas never understood the whole concept and ridiculed it. John remembered when he first brought up the topic.

"What will you do with land in Virginia? You're not going to live there," Thomas said.

John shrugged. "Well, I'm not going to acquire land right now, but we could sell the headrights."

"To whom? No one there has any money. You told me yourself they're doing their best just trying to survive."

"You have a point, brother, but I think I should collect a few, regardless, so I have land to build my own warehouses someday. Paying rent for storehouses in Jamestown is a waste of money."

"And having passengers in place of cargo is also a waste of money," Thomas scoffed.

Thomas was tense and angry that day, but John found out later his brother's angst had nothing to do with headrights. It had been the anniversary of their father's death.

When John first bought his ship and was readying it for his maiden voyage, Thomas appeared at the dockyard and requested John go see their ailing father before he sailed. John refused. John's relationship with his father had always been a strained one, and no matter how much Thomas wanted them to get along, John knew nothing would repair the years of resentment and stubbornness.

John watched Thomas sulk away in frustration that day, wondering if perhaps his brother was right—that John should be a good son and go visit his father. Johannes's home of Astwood Court was nearly a ten-day trip from London and John didn't have that kind of time. He wanted to get his ship out to sea, not waste weeks traveling to see the old man. It would just be the same old arguments. His father would threaten to disown him. John would slink out of the room, beaten. His father would slam something and not speak to him for the next six months. It was a finely tuned dance that John knew all too well.

Johannes's anger wasn't the worst part of their relationship nor the main cause of the pain John felt in his heart. John had always felt ignored by his father and that Thomas was their father's favorite, but what upset him the most was that Johannes had never put business aside for the family. As John matured, he realized that he and his siblings had essentially grown up without a father. The man's excuse was that he was always working, but it wasn't a truthful excuse. Work didn't take the place of family, unless one chose to let it.

When John refused to travel to Astwood Court to visit his father, he'd glimpsed himself doing exactly the same thing his father had always done — choosing work over family. He refused to dwell upon the thought. Johannes Culpepper had wasted twenty-eight years when he could have been spending time with John. If the man died while John was at sea, then so be it.

John knew his brother was disappointed in him, but his anger toward his father was all encompassing and made it impossible for him to feel anything else for the old man. He'd marched back up the gangplank that day, waving his hand behind his back at Thomas to brush him off. He'd hastily climbed aboard his ship to continue overseeing the preparations for his voyage. He never looked back.

John was in Virginia when his father took

his last breath on December 3, 1635.

CHAPTER 8

July 1643, Accomac, Virginia

On this gray and drizzling morning, a dozen local men were busy erecting John's new storehouse in Accomac. The clatter of construction pounded through John's skull as if the men were pounding their hammers directly on his head, which had been throbbing for the last week since he received word from Thomas about the recent incidents in England.

War had escalated greatly, and John's cousin Nicholas had been seen in battle, fighting *against* the king. How could a Culpepper do that? It was unheard of and would surely result in a charge of treason and Nicholas's beheading, not to mention a dark stain on the Culpepper family's good name. Thomas related to John in a letter that he had fought against Nicholas at Newbury. Nicholas had sustained a serious chest injury but Thomas could not stop to help him. He said it didn't look as if any man could survive that kind of injury, and Thomas was certain Nicholas would be dead soon, if he wasn't already.

The letter made John sick to his stomach. He fondly remembered playing with Nicholas as a child and was proud of the work Nicholas had recently done in transcribing the pharmacopeia from Latin to English for the good of all man. How could a man—a gentleman—so upstanding turn against the king? It didn't make any sense. John stood on the side of the muddy building site, closed his eyes, and rubbed his temples in a futile attempt to ease the pain.

That very morning, he had received a second letter, this time from his uncle Alexander. It stated that Nicholas had died from his wounds. John was mortified. Uncle Alexander also related that he was preparing to go to Bolton to muster more men. Apparently, the Scots had marched south and joined the parliamentarian army in York. The war was moving closer and closer to John's family in Kent, and John was stuck with no ship on the other side of the ocean listening to pounding and sawing until he thought his head would explode. His stomach churned. He needed to finish building his warehouse and get back to his wife and sons. He wondered if he could finally convince Mary to sail with him to Virginia and start a new life. Yes, there were skirmishes with the Indians upon occasion, and yes, the amenities were far less than a woman of her breeding was accustomed to, but at least she wouldn't be caught in the middle of a bloody battle between two capable armies that was going to accomplish nothing when all was said and done.

"Hello, John," someone shouted over the hammering.

Startled out of his thoughts, John opened his eyes and turned toward the familiar voice. His frizzy-headed friend from his days at law school was walking toward him. "Will Berkeley? What are you doing here?"

Will smiled as he approached, hand outstretched in greeting. "Apparently I'm now the governor of this fine land."

"You? That's wonderful news. I've been so busy with my family and my business, I haven't kept up with the local affairs. I can't believe no one told me." John shook Will's hand and patted him on the shoulder.

Berkeley pushed his unkempt hair from his face with his sausage-shaped fingers and then ran them down the sides of his mustache. "The king sent me over to see to his business in the colony, which I am happy to do. It's quite a bit more peaceful here in Virginia than it is in England right now, and I'm too old to fight those battles."

"Oh, Will, we're the same age."

"Well, you're not there fighting, either, are you, John?" Berkeley chuckled.

John shrugged. "True. I live mostly on my ship on the quiet ocean and that's the way I like it." He looked toward the working men and rolled his eyes. "Have you any word from home? I heard the Scots have joined with Parliament and the fighting in the north is growing in intensity."

"Yes, I heard there have been numerous skirmishes up there, but fortunately they've all been a good distance from our family homes." Berkeley looked over at the workers. "What are you building here?"

"It's a new storehouse, but all this pounding is giving me an unbelievable headache. Tell me, when did you arrive in Virginia?"

"A few months ago. I was hoping to get over and see you sooner, but I was building myself. I built a plantation about three miles the other side of Jamestown. I called it Green Springs. I kept waiting for you to come back in town so I could come say hello, but then I heard you abandoned Jamestown and took up residence here in Accomac."

"I refuse to pay the tax to dock at

Jamestown."

"I don't blame you. I had to pay the tax when I arrived. Before I left London the king knighted me so I'm officially Sir William Berkeley now." He raised his eyebrows and smiled.

"That's great. Congratulations!"

Berkeley waved off John's comment. "Oh, it's not so great. He's appointing anyone who owns a rusty sword to be a squire for him. Between me and you, I think he's terrified of losing this rebellion."

"From what I've heard from my uncle and my brother, I think you're right."

"How is Thomas? I haven't seen him in ages."

"He's been promoted to colonel in the king's army and is running his law practice at the same time. Last I saw him back in May, his hair was turning a bit gray."

Berkeley laughed. "I told you we're getting old. Anyway, I'd heard that Thomas was promoted and I figured he could deliver a correspondence to the king for me. I came by to see if you're sailing back to London any time soon. I would be happy to pay you for your trouble if you could make the delivery for me."

"I'm actually heading back as soon as my ship returns, probably by November. If it can wait until then, I'll be happy to run that errand for you. My wife is due with our fifth child, so I need to get back before she delivers or she'll have my head on a plate."

"Fifth child? I didn't know you had children."

John nodded and smiled with pride. "Four, all boys."

"What about Thomas? I remember hearing he married just out of law school."

"He married Katherine St. Leger. They have four children also. Two boys and two girls. What about you, Will?"

"No, I never married. Just never found the right woman, I guess."

"You've always been a rogue, Will Berkeley. Perhaps with your new title, you can finally attract a respectable woman."

Berkeley winked. "Only if someone brings one over from England. All the lasses here are spoken for."

"That's true."

"Well, it's obviously been too long since we've seen each other, my friend. We'll have to make plans to go fishing when you return to Virginia."

"Of course!"

Will shook John's hand. "Listen, I must be going, but I wish you and your wife a healthy child, and I trust you won't run into any skirmishes while you're in the homeland. The king has made more than a few enemies in Parliament, but it doesn't matter much to men like us. We'll take care of the king and he will do so in kind."

They walked toward Will's horse and he reached in his saddlebag and removed a large stack of papers tied with a piece of twine. He handed the stack to John. "Please get these to the king for me when you can, and I wish you a safe voyage. I expect you to come out and see my new plantation when you return to Virginia."

"I would love to visit. It's so good to see you, Will, and it's good to know you're here in case I need anything."

"You know I'll help in any way I can, and I can't thank you enough for delivering my messages to the king."

"I'll see to it personally."

CHAPTER 9

January 1644, Greenway Court

On a blustery, cold January morning, John docked in London. He went straight to his brother's office to deliver Berkeley's documents.

Thomas greeted him with a hug and a huge smile. "John, I'm so glad you're home."

"I have a favor to ask of you. Will you deliver these documents to the king for Will Berkeley?"

"Berkeley? Where did you run into him?"

"He's the new governor of Virginia. I was in the middle of building the warehouse on my new property when he appeared out of nowhere."

"Well, that must have been quite a

surprise. I haven't seen him in ages."

"Those are the exact words he said about you, too. He looks the same, except for a few more pounds around the middle. Indeed it was a surprise when he appeared like that, but I would have known him anywhere with that frizzy hair." John handed the stack of papers to Thomas. "He asked if we'd deliver these to the king and I told him we would see to it."

As the brothers were catching up on all the news from Virginia and the happenings in England, the stable boy from Greenway Court ran into the office and informed John and Thomas that Mary was having her baby. On the four-hour journey to Greenway Court, the boy told John that Mary had gone into labor early that morning, at which time he was sent to London to inform Thomas. They didn't know John was back in the country.

The birth took so long, John arrived home long before the child was born. He paced across the stone floor of the dining room for hours before Katherine finally descended the stairs, exhausted but smiling.

"John, Mary has delivered you another son."

"Is she all right?"

"Yes. The birth was long, but she and the babe are well."

John marched up the stairs, taking them two at a time, and opened the heavy door without knocking.

"Mary, are you all right?" he whispered.

She leaned back on a stack of pillows, looking fatigued and very pale, but she reached her hand out for him. "John. Yes, I'm tired but all right. I'm glad you're home."

"I told you I would be back in time." He flew across the room and took her hand, raising it to his lips.

She smiled. "You've always been a man of your word."

"As long as you don't have early babies, I'll always be here." He grinned and kissed her on the top of her head. He pulled up a chair and looked at the bundle in her arms. "May I see him?"

"Of course." She laid the babe on the bed and removed his wraps.

John examined his new son. The typical brown curly hair and blue eyes met with his approval. They wrapped him back up and placed him next to his mother. She snuggled down in the bed, looking drowsy. Soon Mary and the babe fell asleep and John went downstairs to let them rest. With all the excitement, they had missed lunch and the evening sun was melting into the horizon as Katherine asked the kitchen girl to make them some warm cider and plates of food. John sat down with Katherine and Thomas at the dining room table.

"Congratulations on another healthy boy, John," Katherine said.

"Thank you for being here to deliver the baby," John said.

"Of course. Where else would I be? What will you name him?"

John looked across the table at Thomas. "Perhaps John, after our grandfather."

"John Culpepper is a good name." Katherine giggled. "But between you, JC, and our young JJ, you'll have to come up with something else to call him. We have far too many Johns around here. Perhaps you can call him Johnny." She swiped a wisp of auburn hair back from her forehead with her palm, her emerald eyes twinkling in the candlelight.

John admired his sister-in-law who was stunningly beautiful, even with the dark circles under her eyes. "Yes, that's a good idea. Johnny it is." His face softened with compassion as he watched her. "You must be exhausted, Katherine."

Katherine nodded as the kitchen girl filled her cup. She took a sip of the cider and sighed. "I'm not as tired as your wife. She had quite a time of it, but she'll be fine in a few days."

"I know she's extremely grateful to have you with her."

"I'm glad to be with her. She's like a sister to me."

"Thank you for welcoming my family

into your home." John glanced from Katherine to Thomas. "Both of you."

"We wouldn't have it any other way, John," Thomas said.

John looked around the room. "Where are the children?"

"I sent the older ones down to the stables," Thomas said. "And the governess took the younger ones for a walk in the garden and just brought them in while you were with Mary. The fresh air always puts them right to sleep."

John looked down at his cup and thought of his sons and how anxious he was to see them. It felt unbelievable that he had docked only that morning. It seemed like weeks ago.

"Where are we going to put a crib?" John asked.

Katherine laughed. "I don't know. We're running out of space in the nursery. Maybe we'll have to move one of the boys into his own room."

With John's four sons and Thomas and Katherine's four children, all between the ages of three and fourteen, the house was filled with squeals and cries nearly all the time, and this was a rare quiet moment.

Katherine changed the subject. "I always thought Henry looked so much like you, but this baby resembles you even more. All of your boys have that same dark curly hair." She looked down, and John could tell she wasn't picturing the children's cherub faces. Her face had turned dark. "She misses you so much when you're not here. So do the boys."

"I miss them, too."

"It's very dreary without you, John." She took a sip and sighed again. "There's nothing we can do in your absence but pray for your safe return."

John didn't know how to respond. He had been on the sea for the last decade, making his living. He didn't know how he could change that, and truthfully, he didn't want to.

Thomas broke the awkwardness. "Well, I'll go out to the stables and find the children. I'll be right back."

Katherine and John sat in silence. She seemed near exhaustion. He was in deep thought over her comment.

Katherine's brow furrowed. "Do you think the uprising is going to come down this far? The thought of our children being in danger terrifies me."

"It frightens me, too. My heart wants to tell you war will never come down this far, that things will be just fine, but from everything I've heard from Thomas and in town, I think this war is going to spread throughout the whole country eventually."

"What are we going to do?" Katherine drank the last of her cider and set her cup down. "Do you think we're safe here?"

"We're safe out here in the country for now. But if the winds of fortune should change, it's a good thing we know someone who owns a ship, isn't it?" He smiled at her, trying to ease the tension, but the lines in her forehead deepened.

At that moment, three-year-old Robbie wailed from upstairs in his crib, immediately followed by Thomas and the children bursting through the back door, hollering about what they'd just seen at the stables.

Their quiet time had abruptly ended.

CHAPTER 10

1644, Boys

The next morning, following a hearty breakfast, John climbed the stairs, followed by his rambunctious sons, all wanting to see the new baby. He cracked the door open and found Mary sitting up in bed holding the newborn, her brown hair cascading over her shoulders. Her color was much better after a good night's sleep.

"Your sons want to see the baby," John whispered almost apologetically.

"Of course they do. Bring them in."

John opened the door and the group ran toward the bed. Mary grinned at them and patted the bed for Robbie to climb up. John thought his wife was a saint, or at least had the patience of one.

All the boys looked like their father, but none more so than the new baby. The boys cooed over the infant, and John reminded them repeatedly to keep their voices down. It was a wasted request.

"He looks like you!" Denny exclaimed, looking at Henry.

"What are you saying? That I look like a baby?" Henry challenged.

The baby scrunched up his face at the sound of the voices.

James laughed. "I've seen you make that face. He does look just like you."

Henry punched him in the arm and James punched back.

"Stop it," John scolded.

Mary looked down the row of children lining her bedside. "Well, I think all my boys look like their handsome father."

"You're handsome," teased Denny, punching James in the arm.

"No, you're handsome," James punched back.

"All right, let's go and let your mother rest." John picked up Robbie and coaxed the rest of the herd toward the door. Denny and James began poking each other. John handed three-year-old Robbie to Henry and grabbed both misbehavers by their hair.

"Ouch," they squealed in unison.

"I told you to be quiet and stop acting like…"

"Acting like what?" Denny said in defiance.

"Well…boys. Stop acting like boys." John laughed at his own lack of parenting skills. Four years of law school, a momentary career as a lawyer, and a decade of commanding a boisterous crew on a merchant ship were no preparation for raising high-spirited boys. He thought about it for a moment and realized that besides his younger sister Frances, who was now a thirty-six-year-old married woman, he had always been the youngest of his generation. He'd never had any younger brothers or cousins to mind. One thing was for certain — Mary had her hands full during John's lengthy absences, and he suddenly understood why she often pleaded with him to remain home for longer stretches of time. He was exhausted and it was only nine o'clock in the morning.

* * *

The following evening, John shared supper with Mary alone in the quiet of her room, and she again brought up the subject of his absences.

"Can't you just stay home for another month? Why do you have to go back so soon?"

"Dearest, I am already scheduled to take

some settlers to Virginia in a few weeks. I'm receiving cash as well as their headrights. We'll have quite a bit of land at our disposal in Virginia should we ever need it. I'm sorry, but I can't postpone this voyage."

She looked as if she were about to cry. She always became tearful after birthing a child. He knew her intense emotions would cease in a few weeks, but the knowledge of it didn't make it any better right now when she looked so sad.

She looked down at the babe in her arms and a single tear dropped onto the infant's blanket. John knelt on the floor and looked up at her. "I give you my word, I will come straight home. I won't tarry in Virginia any longer than necessary."

Her lip began to quiver.

"What is it, my dear? What is making you so sad?" John asked.

Her eyes brimmed with a multitude of tears that threatened to spill over. "I'm just growing more and more frightened for our children. We're living in the middle of a war, John."

"Thomas and Uncle Alexander are taking great care to keep you and the children safe, and I trust them."

"I know you do. I do, too, but Katherine is beside herself with worry also. Thomas doesn't come home for months at a time, and we never know if he's still alive or lying dead on some battlefield. Uncle Alexander is riding around the countryside mustering more men. God forbid, what if one of them doesn't come back?"

John rose from his knees and sat down on the edge of her bed. "Mary, you're worrying yourself needlessly. You are more than safe here. Culpeppers have always worked in the service of the king, and the king will make sure we're taken care of and well kept."

Thomas's twelve-year-old son, Alex, and Henry barged through the door at that moment, waving wooden sticks at each other.

"En garde!" yelled Henry.

"En garde!" hollered Alex.

John stood up. "Boys, boys, boys. Take your battle outside."

Henry stopped and faced his father. "But, Father, Anna and Frances are playing outside and they want us to be their squires and wait on them."

Alex chimed in. "And Frances says she's the queen and Henry should be her king and save her from the Scots."

"I don't care if the Scots themselves are outside. Take your sticks and your yelling and go downstairs. You're going to wake up the baby." John ushered the boys out the door and closed it. He turned and leaned his back on the door, looking at his beautiful wife across the candle-lit room. "Boys," he sighed.

"See what I mean? Even the children are

playing war."

"I understand." As he returned to her side, he glanced out the window and noticed his uncle galloping toward the house on his white stallion. "It looks like Uncle Alexander has returned. I'll speak with him before I leave and find out exactly where the battle lines are being drawn. I won't leave you in danger, Mary. I promise." He paused. "You do have a choice, though."

"What's that?"

"You could sail with me to Virginia. We could make a new home there."

"No, I'm not taking the boys on the ship. It's too dangerous."

"Compared to living in the middle of a war? You know my ship is not dangerous. It's well provisioned and my crew is well trained."

"Nevertheless, I don't want to sail to Virginia. This is our home. I don't want to leave it."

John sat on the edge of the bed and gently rubbed his hand across Mary's hair. When she closed her eyes and he knew she was relaxed, he took Johnny from her arms and placed him in the cradle. He then crawled under the quilt next to his wife and held her as she fell asleep.

He hoped she and the boys would never have to leave their home, but he was almost certain they would have to eventually. In Virginia, he had started building himself a small two-room house. Perhaps he should make it larger to accommodate his family. He would hate to see the concern on Mary's face when they were forced to take the boys on the ship. He would really hate to see it when they arrived in Virginia and she found out they'd have to live in squalor.

CHAPTER 11

May 1645, Sir Alexander Culpepper

John prepared himself to leave for Virginia as scheduled. His ship was well provisioned, the passengers had been notified of the sailing date, and his crew was at the ready. He traveled home for a few days to pack his belongings. He stood on the back terrace under the morning's cloudless sky and shook the dust and sea salt from his black woolen coat. The bright sunlight painted stark shadows beneath the trees and on the side of the barn. John glanced at the barn and saw his uncle Alexander, dressed in full military gear, talking to the stable boy. John placed his coat on a chair and walked across the yard toward them.

"Good morning, Uncle. Are you returning to the king?"

"Good morning, John. No, the king is in good hands. I'm heading to Bridgewater to meet up with our friend George Goring."

"Goring is back? I thought he was out of the country trying to garner support for the king."

"He came back last summer and has amassed quite a large army."

"What's happening at Bridgewater?"

"The town of Taunton, which has been our main supply line in the south, was seized last summer by Cromwell's army, and the king ordered Goring to move his men south and take the town back. Unfortunately, the thorn in my side, General Thomas Fairfax, appeared with nearly a thousand troops and stopped Goring in his tracks. Goring lost a lot of men in the battle and had no choice but to retreat to Bridgewater. His messenger sent word that they're trying to protect the retreat of the baggage and artillery, so his army is spread out over twelve miles, from Langport to Yeovil. You know how slow moving artillery can be."

John didn't know, but he nodded.

"Cromwell and Fairfax have a cavalry regiment and four infantry regiments tailing Goring, and Goring's men are outnumbered two to one. I'm going to round up my men and head to Bridgewater to help."

"Will there be a battle?" John took a deep breath, willing himself to remain calm. The fighting was now in the south. How long would it be before it reached Kent?

"More than likely, yes, there will be a considerable battle." Alexander tightened his saddle.

"Is Thomas there?" John heard the quiver in his own voice.

"No, the last I heard, he was at Uxbridge. The king's commissioners met with Parliament's commissioners to negotiate an end to this damn war." Alexander stopped moving for a moment. "I know what a talented lawyer your brother is, and I'm sure he did the best he could, but I heard the negotiations ended unsuccessfully. Between futile negotiations and losing our supply line in Taunton, I'm afraid we need to create some victories or we're going to lose this war. The first thing we need to do is get Taunton back, but I need to get Goring out of Bridgewater first."

John didn't know what to say or do. His heart was pounding. His hands were sweating. He needed to get to his ship and sail to Virginia. He needed to stay in Kent and defend his family. He needed a drink of ale. "Do you need me to go with you?"

Alexander shook his head as he tied his bedroll to the back of the saddle. "No, John, you're not a trained military man. You need to watch after your ship in case we're not successful."

"My ship?"

"I know you fought your father over buying that ship, and I know how stubborn that man could be. It was a brave thing you did, standing up to him." He grunted as he pulled the leather straps tightly around the horse. "If we lose this war, you're going to need that ship to get your family out of here. It may be the only thing between your family's safety and your brother's head on a spike."

The sights, sounds, and smells of the barn swirled around John's head. For a moment, he felt as if he might faint. The sunny day he enjoyed only moments ago swam before his eyes and his throat constricted, making it difficult to get his next breath. He stood motionless as he watched the stable boy and Uncle Alexander move at lightning speed, ignoring him. They tied supplies to the white horse. They checked the buckles and the ties. Their movements were precise.

Alexander stopped moving and looked over the horse's back at John. "John, if I don't return from Bridgewater..."

John shook his head. "You always return, Uncle."

"Well, if I don't, I need you to know I've changed my will. Remember when Alex was born, I left Leeds Castle in keeping to him? I've changed the will to read that the castle belongs to Alex only as long as Thomas is alive to oversee it. I don't know that Alex is equipped to handle such an inheritance by himself. If anything happens to your brother, the castle will go to JC. JC will decide what to do with it."

"I don't want to hear you speak of such things. Alex doesn't need a castle."

"No one *needs* a castle, but this is important. If things don't go as planned and this war ends in Parliament's favor, they will try to seize all of our property, including Greenway Court. They'll try to take Leeds Castle, too, so I'm asking you to keep my will in a safe place so you can prove that I left the castle to Alex. He's a minor, so they can't touch it if it belongs to him, and you're a lawyer, so I know you can handle this."

"I'm not a lawyer."

Alexander swiftly mounted his horse. The stable boy backed away. Alexander looked down at John as the horse began prancing in circles. "Yes, you are, and a damn good one—just as your father always wanted you to be." He cleared his throat. "I think we're losing this war, John, and when that happens, they'll take everything our family has worked so hard for. They *will* take Greenway Court because of your brother's loyalties, and you must remain alert in case you need to get your family away from here."

John nodded. "Should I take them to Virginia?"

"If we lose this war, it doesn't matter where you take them, but you need to take them somewhere quickly and under the cloak of darkness. Cromwell will search out anyone who has sided with the king. They will be charged as traitors and more than likely beheaded. You need to watch over your brother."

"What about you?"

"There's nothing you can do for me. I'll be long dead before this war ends."

"Nonsense. You don't really think the future is that grim, do you?"

"I *know* it's that grim. You need to care for your children and Thomas's children. If we fail, you get them to safety as quickly as you can. Upon my honor, I will gladly give my life to keep the rightful king on the throne, and I shall willingly die by the sword of my enemy before I see our country in the hands of Cromwell."

Without a good-bye, Uncle Alexander galloped off in a thunder of hooves and a trail of dust, leaving John standing in the middle of the yard, pale and shaken.

CHAPTER 12

July 1645, Battle at Bridgewater

Alexander Culpepper appeared on the scene with sixty men on horseback. Most were dressed in their finest armor, but some were merely farmers whom Alexander had persuaded to join the efforts against the parliamentarians. He climbed down from his horse and found George Goring in a tent in the middle of the royalists' temporary camp.

He removed his hat and gave George a sweeping bow. "Lord Goring, I am at your service."

Goring looked up from the maps strewn across the table. "Alexander, so nice of you to join us. How many men did you bring?"

"Sixty men on horse."

"That is good news." Goring pointed to the maps and gestured for Alexander to come closer. Over the next hour, he pointed out the locations of Fairfax's men and explained the plan of attack. He expected the battle to take place within the next few days. "It's taken us a month to get here because our baggage and artillery were moving so slowly. I've been forced to keep my strongest defenses in the rear because Fairfax has been in pursuit every inch of the way. Fairfax engaged us at Yeovil and took the town and a large portion of my artillery, but we moved as quickly as we could and crossed to the north side of the River Yeo and have stayed ahead of him since then. I located a viable place on this ridge and decided to stop here and let him catch up. From this vantage point, we will be able to defeat him once and for all. Fairfax's days are numbered."

"I hope so. As I was gathering my men, I heard we took a bad defeat in Naseby, and Leicester surrendered only days later."

"Well, we won't take a defeat here. This will be our deciding victory over these damn parliamentarians." Goring pointed to the map. "This ridge we're on runs north and south and my men are spread out across the top of it. Fairfax is sitting to the east of it. Between us is nothing but marsh and in front of that is a stream. Since we've seen rain nearly every day for the last month, there's only one dry place to cross. Fairfax will either take the dry ford across the stream or he'll have to maneuver around us, which will take him days and allow us even more time to prepare. Either way, we're in good shape. I have two light guns on top of the ridge, guarding the ford that crosses the stream. There isn't another way around the water for miles. They'll have to come across right there. I also have Welsh foot soldiers in the marsh, lying in wait in the trees and bushes on either side of the ford, prepared to engage Fairfax's men when they cross the stream. And now with your men, we have three bodies of horse to destroy them if they manage to get past the light guns and the foot soldiers."

"It's a good plan. After we take out Fairfax, we can move back south and recapture Taunton. I'd like to battle Cromwell and be the first to put my sword in his heart."

"I left some men to create a diversion in Taunton so he's still there. I didn't want him coming north with Fairfax. I don't have enough men to fight them both."

"At least we'll get Fairfax."

"Yes, we will."

* * *

Four days later, a messenger came to Alexander's tent in the wee hours of the morning and told him Fairfax's army had appeared, ten thousand strong. Alexander crawled out of his tent, stomped through the mud, and donned his armor. He saddled his horse and rode his men to the top of the ridge, where they waited for the battle to begin. Ten thousand men would be no easy task, but the battle was well planned. Alexander's and Goring's armies would be victorious on this day.

Alexander noticed movement in the bushes below. He knew the Welsh foot soldiers were lying in wait for Fairfax, so he didn't concern himself with the movement. Then he heard the first musket shot and the first scream. The Welsh soldiers emerged from the bushes as if they were on fire. They were in hand-to-hand combat with Fairfax's men. They were armed with matchlock muskets, but the guns were useless with the enemy right on top of them.

Alexander's chest constricted in confusion. He wasn't sure what was happening below, but as he saw the Welsh soldiers falling at an alarming rate, he deduced that somehow Fairfax's men had crossed the stream unnoticed. The sounds of shouts and clangs of swords rose up the ridge, and Alexander knew the men were fighting for their lives. He looked down the row of horses toward Goring. Goring was looking down the ridge in disbelief at the carnage. Goring's face, usually an expression of stone, changed in an instant. His jaw fell open, his eyes widened in horror. This didn't make Alexander feel any better. The men below were outnumbered by at least three thousand. Losing the Welsh soldiers at the very beginning of the battle would be a devastating blow.

"Fire the light guns!" Goring commanded.

The cannon fire would hit not only the enemy, but also the Welsh soldiers. From the looks of it, the soldiers would all be dead soon regardless.

The light guns prepared to fire, but Fairfax's artillery rang out from either side of them. In a flash of flying dirt and screaming men, both of Goring's guns were taken out within moments of each other. How did Fairfax's men surround the ridge with cannons in tow? How did they arrive unseen and unheard? Didn't Goring have sentries posted? The Welsh soldiers who had been hiding in the bushes were now lying in pools of blood. The light guns and the men arming them were now scattered across the ridge like rag dolls. Goring looked down the line and slowly shook his head at Alexander.

Goring then yelled to his men, "Advance the first cavalry!"

Goring and Alexander remained on the top of the ridge and watched the first group of horses gallop down the hill through gun and cannon fire. Dirt and debris flew as Fairfax's cannons fired down upon them. Some men were taken from their horses, and the horses galloped around in circles with no rider to lead them. The battle was becoming a mass of confusion.

"Advance the second cavalry!" Goring commanded.

The second group galloped down the hill.

That's when Alexander saw them on the other side of the stream. Fairfax's cavalry appeared out of nowhere, crossing the ford with nothing to stop their advance. There was no clanging of armor as with a regular group of horse heading into battle. Alexander knew these soldiers weren't in armor. The weight would slow down the horses. He had to admit, Fairfax was a brilliant commander. There was no thunder of hooves as the horses were not galloping. The approaching men were dressed in leather jerkins and moved to a strange and ominous sound of marching hooves and creaking leather. A menacing sound sure to make even the most courageous opponent question his bravery.

They advanced four abreast, knee to knee, with four more behind, and four more behind that. There had to be hundreds of them. They looked like demons rising from the very depths of hell, bent on killing each and every royalist. What happened to the day of fighting with honor and valor? When did the parliamentarians stop taking prisoners? When did they start killing every man who crossed their path? The Welsh soldiers were gone. The light guns were gone. The only thing standing between success and defeat were the three groups of horse, two of which were not faring so well against Fairfax's army.

"Ready your swords, gentlemen!" Alexander yelled to his men who were waiting nervously at the top of the ridge. Nearly half his men were not professional soldiers but farmers. They weren't used to facing anything this terrifying. He wasn't sure *he* had ever faced anything this terrifying. "Steady..." He watched the horses below him advance across the ford, and far in the distance, he recognized a figure dressed all in black astride a white horse. Fairfax. Black Tom, the royalists called him. The man sat tall in his saddle at the back of his army, looking like Satan himself. Alexander felt his adrenaline rise. Today would be the day General Thomas Fairfax paid for his decision to abandon the king's men. Today would be the day Black Tom took a sword through his black heart.

Alexander's men waited and watched, their horses prancing nervously. Fairfax's group of horses easily destroyed Goring's first line, scattering the men about the marsh like scarecrows. Even horses lay dead. Alexander grimaced as he watched more men fall and some of the horses run off. The second group fought more diligently than the first and Alexander thought for a moment they could win the battle. That's when he saw the next group of Fairfax's men on horseback, larger than the first, crossing the stream, again four abreast. There had to be more than two hundred of them.

"Ready, men!" He yelled to his group of sixty men.

Their swords glistened in the sunlight. This would be the day of their greatest victory or their worst defeat.

Alexander took a deep breath, braced himself, and from the pit of his stomach he bellowed, "Charge!"

CHAPTER 13

July 28, 1645, Accomac

John had been in Virginia for almost two weeks and was anxious to provision his ship and sail back home, but the general assembly had summoned him to be a witness in a dispute between his friend Anthony Hodgkins and the town troublemaker, Sir Edmund Plowden. John had had more than one run-in with Plowden over the last fifteen years and didn't look forward to seeing the man again. He especially didn't appreciate the fact that he was stuck in Virginia because of Plowden when he should be on his way home to see to the safety of his wife and children.

He sat on the steps outside the Tan House

in Nassawadox and awaited his summons. The tan-colored house, hence the name, was located on the peninsula twenty miles south of Accomac and was used for all matters of law and colonial business. It was also the gathering place for social events, used as a tavern on regular days. Today was not a regular day. Today was the day they held court.

"John Culpepper, please come in," called the clerk from the door.

John rose and entered the Tan House, not much more than a one-room shack. He marched to the front of the room, his boots clunking on the wooden floor, and he took a seat in front of the members of the court. The magistrate instructed Plowden's lawyer to come forward to question John.

"Mr. Culpepper, the storehouse in Accomac that Sir Edmund Plowden agreed to rent is owned by you, correct?" asked the lawyer.

"Yes, sir."

"When did you agree to rent it to Sir Edmund?"

"Last summer."

"And what were the terms for the rental?"

"The agreement was for him to rent the rear half of my storehouse and build a partition, which was to be paid for out of his own pocket. Sir Edmund made an agreement with Anthony

Hodgkins to build the partition, but Mr. Hodgkins couldn't finish it on time."

"And why not?"

"He said after the trees were felled, it rained heavily for seven days and the oxen couldn't pull the timber to the site. When Sir Edmund returned and found the partition not finished, he lost his temper and wouldn't listen to the legitimate excuse. He threatened Mr. Hodgkins with court proceedings and refused to pay him for the work he had already done."

"So, Mr. Hodgkins never finished the partition?"

"No, he didn't. I advised Mr. Hodgkins to stop working on the partition because I knew he would never get paid."

"You advised this?"

"Yes, sir. It's my storehouse, so Mr. Hodgkins is not allowed on the premises unless I allowed him to be. Therefore, it was not his fault the partition wasn't finished. I immediately broke the lease with Sir Edmund to end the transaction without Mr. Hodgkins being financially hurt any further."

"How was Mr. Hodgkins hurt financially?"

"He hadn't been paid for the work he had done up until that point, and judging from Sir Edmund's reputation, Mr. Hodgkins probably wouldn't be paid even if he did finish the partition."

"Sir Edmund is not on trial here, Mr. Culpepper."

"He should be. He's a violent man of unfortunate personality who is currently involved in no less than forty other legal proceedings in Elizabeth City and York County, including charges of forgery and assault. Mr. Hodgkins was not paid for a partition which he did not build because he was not allowed on the property at the insistence of the building owner, namely me. Plowden did not suffer any damages by the incident. At the most, he was inconvenienced by a few months of time. I don't understand why this court is wasting its time with the likes of Edmund Plowden and his trivial suits. He is scum and worth nothing more than a yeasty codpiece."

The courtroom erupted into shouts and laughter and the magistrate slammed his gavel over and over, shouting for order.

* * *

After the charges against Anthony Hodgkins were dismissed, John invited Anthony and Nathaniel Littleton to the nearby tavern for an ale in celebration of the victory. Anthony thanked John profusely.

"You don't need to thank me, Anthony. Somebody should run Plowden out of town. The more people find out what a bully he is, the less likely he is to stay."

"What did he ever do that was so bad?" Anthony asked as he sipped his ale.

"What *hasn't* he done is more like it. He's facing charges for a land grant he said he was given for New Albion, but the grant was forged. He's a dishonest man and a drunkard. He's been arrested dozens of times for assault and destruction of property while intoxicated."

"Then why did you rent your storehouse to him?"

"I didn't realize who he was at the time. I had never met him before, but I met his wife back in England. When I worked as a lawyer in London, a woman named Mabel Plowden came to me, asking me to represent her against her abusive husband. She said he demanded that she sell the estate she had brought into the marriage so he could have the money, and when she refused, he became excessively cruel. The first time she came to my office, she was great with child and had bruises all over her. I thought she needed more help than I could give her, so I referred her to the archbishop of Canterbury, who thought her case had enough merit to be brought before the high commissioners. Her husband got scared that he would get into trouble for beating his wife, so he groveled to the archbishop, agreeing to treat her better, and she reluctantly returned home with him."

"So, Edmund Plowden's a wife beater,

too?" asked Anthony.

John nodded. "And a violent one at that. What kind of man beats his pregnant wife?" He turned and spit on the sawdust floor. "But that's not the end of the story. A year later, she came forward again, and this time she sued him for divorce."

"Divorce?"

"She said he had lied to the archbishop. He'd never stopped beating her and the violence was escalating. When she appeared before the high commissioners with a black eye, Plowden was imprisoned for assault, but the day they took him from the jail to the court to face the charges, he escaped from the guards. Without him present in the courtroom, the commissioners charged him with paying her alimony for the rest of her life, but he had already fled to Virginia to avoid the charges and paying her."

"Where is she now?" Littleton asked.

"I assume she's still living in Kent. And he's here causing trouble." John shook his head at Anthony. "But don't worry about him. He's not a real man. A real man wouldn't beat his wife then run away like a scurvy dog when confronted. He won't cause you any more trouble, Anthony. I'll guarantee that."

"I saw him give you a dirty look when he left the courtroom," said Anthony.

John blew a puff of air between his lips.

"I'm not worried about him. His dirty looks don't concern me in the least."

"Well, someone should teach him a lesson," Anthony said.

"Someday, someone will," Littleton said. "But I prefer to stay far away from someone like that. If you roll around in the rubbish pile, you will undoubtedly get some of it on you. It's not worth it. He's not worth it."

"No truer statement has ever been spoken. I'm sorry I ever rented my storehouse to him, and I'm sorry you got involved with him, Anthony."

"That's all right. I've learned my lesson, and thank you again for coming to my rescue." Anthony raised his glass to John, who returned the gesture.

John turned to Nathaniel. "Have you gotten any word from home lately? The war seemed to be escalating fast when I left."

"Yes, as a matter of fact, I received a letter just this morning. My family wrote that there were deadly skirmishes in Taunton and Bridgewater, both lost to the hands of Parliament."

John's stomach tightened. "My uncle was at Bridgewater. I hope he's all right." John looked down into his mug. "I'm nervous that the fighting has moved into the south, but I'm sure my brother is seeing to my family." He looked at Anthony. "My brother is now a colonel in the king's army so we stand to lose everything if Parliament wins. My uncle told me Parliament could go so far as to seize our lands and even arrest us on charges of treason."

"How can one be charged with treason while fighting *with* the king?" Nathaniel asked.

John shook his head. "I know. I don't understand it either. It doesn't make any sense. I don't know what those parliamentarians are thinking, but I know there's no end to what they will do to win this war and dethrone the king." John wiped his mouth with the back of his hand. "I'm worried about my wife and sons."

"How many boys do you have?" Anthony asked.

"Five."

"Are you going to bring them here someday?"

"My wife won't let me. I've tried to get her on board the ship, but she refuses. In the meantime, my brother is in charge of their keeping so they're in good hands."

"Sounds like a nice family. I'm sure you miss them. I know I miss my family," Anthony said.

John finished his mug of ale. "Yes, I do miss them. I'm sailing back as soon as I can get my ship ready, maybe tomorrow or the day after."

Nathaniel straightened up in his chair as if he just remembered something. "Oh! Make sure you stop by Henry Pedenden's before you go. He wanted to speak to you about bringing over some members of his family."

"I don't think I'll have room this time, but I'll make sure to speak with him next time." John waved at the barmaid for a refill.

CHAPTER 14

October 1645, All Saints Church

Following the reading of Sir Alexander Culpepper's will at Leeds Castle, Thomas took John out to visit their uncle's tomb at All Saints Church. The day was white and plain, the sky covered in a gauze of clouds that would not allow the sun to shine through. John stared down at his horse's mane, allowing it to follow Thomas's horse without coaxing. The brothers rode in silence the entire way, Thomas grieving his dead uncle, John lost in his thoughts that were far deeper and more painful than losing Uncle Alexander.

As they neared the medieval-looking stone building, it rose majestically before them.

Its central tower featured square parapets that resembled a castle's roof line. John dismounted and paused next to his horse, taking a deep breath. Was he ready to do this? Yes, he needed to pay his respects.

He was devastated by his uncle's death at Bridgewater, but Goring came to see them and told them Alexander died a hero, a brave and valiant knight in His Majesty's service. Uncle Alexander gave his life for a cause he believed in. He was the bravest man John had ever known and John's heart swelled with pride at the courage his uncle had displayed and the sacrifice he had given. John would deal with the rest of his feelings after visiting his uncle's tomb.

John stood next to his horse, unable to convince his legs to walk toward the church. His mind swirled around the memories of ten years earlier when Johannes Culpeper had died while John was away on his very first voyage. When John returned to England and received word of his father's death, he felt anger and resentment, the very same feelings he'd felt when the man was alive, the very same feelings he felt today. The one thing he didn't feel was sadness. He had never before ridden out to this church to visit his father's tomb. This would be his first time seeing it. He felt apprehensive and chastised himself for the feelings. How could his dead father bring up the same feelings now as when John was a boy? How did the man still have control over him from the grave?

"You coming?" Thomas asked from the door.

John nodded and Thomas allowed the door to close as he entered the church. John willed his legs to walk away from his horse. One step at a time. He reached the front door and stopped, reaching over to rub the family crest chiseled in stone to the left of the door. The Culpepper family had been in Kent for many generations and had donated untold amounts of money to this church. A few family members were buried here, dating back over fifty years. There was even a chapel in the building named for the family.

John pulled open the heavy door that moaned in protest on its rusted hinges and he paused, allowing his eyes to adjust to the dim interior. The church was silent. The nave sat before him, adjoined by the chancellery to his right and the vestry to his left. Thomas was walking up the aisle to the place where Uncle Alexander had been laid to rest. John followed.

After staring at the tomb for a few moments, they silently walked to the back of the empty church and sat down in the last pew. They stared straight ahead at the lit candles that graced the altar and the large cross that hung above it.

"Should we have an epitaph made for him?" Thomas asked.

"I guess that would be the appropriate thing to do. I don't know what it should say, though."

"Did you see the one he had made for our father? It's very nice."

John shook his head slightly. "I never came out here to look at it."

Memories of returning to London following his father's death flooded John's mind. The family knew John wouldn't be able to return from Virginia until the weather broke, so they buried Johannes in December and had the reading of the will in January, without John present. The only thing Johannes left his second son was thirty pounds sterling, paid annually by John's cousin JC.

JC had been knighted by King James in 1621 and had sold the family's Wigsell Manor to finance his jaunts around the country. He owed John and Thomas a portion of the proceeds, but since JC had just married and had a wife to support when Johannes fell ill, Johannes negotiated a deal with him to pay the boys an annual income for their lifetimes instead of coming up with all the money at once. Ten years later, JC was now a baron under King Charles, and John had yet to see a single shilling from his cousin. By the time John returned to London in springtime of 1636, Johannes's will and property had all been settled. Just as in life, John didn't receive much from his father in death.

He now sat quietly in the cool, damp church and looked around the nave, wondering where his father's tomb was, wanting to know yet not wanting to know. He thought he should feel sad or tearful or something for his father, but right now he felt nothing but anger for the man.

"Do you know where Father's tomb is?" Thomas asked.

John shook his head.

"It's right over there." Thomas pointed to the left side of the church.

John stared in the general direction. After a few minutes, he reluctantly rose to go look at it.

He weaved through the pews, located his father's tomb, and ran his finger across the chiseled epitaph as he read it.

> *Johannes Culpepper of Feckenham, Armiger.*
> *Second son of John Culpepper of Wigsell.*
> *Died December the year of our Lord 1635,*
> *age 70.*
> *Husband of Ursula Woodcock.*
> *Father of Thomas, Cicely, John, and Frances.*

John stared at the words for a long time. They made his father out to be a good family man. John didn't know that man. He turned, walked back to the pew, and sat down next to his brother.

"Are you all right?" Thomas asked.

John nodded, staring straight ahead.

He couldn't concentrate on the loss of his uncle. He was buried in waves of anger and bitterness over his father. He wanted to shed a tear for him—after all, shouldn't a boy cry when he loses his hero? But he couldn't bring himself to do so. Johannes wasn't a hero.

John was only six when his mother died. He remembered that day very well and he grieved over the loss of her until this day. The governess had broken the news of his mother's death to him and his siblings. His father was too involved with himself to even tell his children their mother had died. Later John was told by his governess that his father was not the cold, callused man John thought him to be. She had known Johannes most of his life and knew John's father never would have had the courage to tell his children something so awful. So, Johannes was nothing more than a coward. He couldn't face the truth so he couldn't bring himself to face his own children at the moment they needed him most. Was that supposed to make John feel better?

As far back as John could remember, his father had been a prominent lawyer in London, then became the sheriff of Warwickshire. The man worked day and night and was seldom home. Even when he was home, he wasn't really there. He spent most of his time in the barn and his mind was always on his work. He was determined for his sons to grow up and become lawyers, too, and had sent the boys away to Middle Temple to study law. John was only fifteen at the time. Thomas was nineteen and emerged from the school with shining credentials. He served as an apprentice for a few prominent lawyers and eventually started his own law practice. John tried to make his father happy by finishing school and playing the role of lawyer for a few years, but he hated every moment of it and it never made his father happy anyway. Nothing could make that man happy.

The only thing John had wanted to do since he was a child was command a ship. When he was twenty, he went to his father and asked for financing to purchase a ship. He was told in no uncertain terms that he would be disowned if he found a way to buy one. Indeed, purchasing his ship was the final nail in the coffin of John's relationship with his father. Johannes never spoke to him again, and the lack of any substantial inheritance, though certainly not a surprise, was the final blow to John's heart. Even from the grave, the man was cold and callused. The governess must have been talking about a different man than the one John knew. But she was right about one thing—the man was a coward.

John wanted to say all these things out loud but couldn't bring himself to do that, either, especially not to Thomas. Thomas seemed to have had a different relationship with their father. He'd loved the man and always stood up for him when John said negative things. Thomas repeatedly told John his feelings toward Johannes were wrong. Maybe Thomas and the governess knew a man John didn't know. John remained silent in the pew. He didn't want to argue with Thomas. Not today.

He rose and left the church, leaving his brother sitting alone.

CHAPTER 15

September 1646, Henry Pedenden

A year had passed since Uncle Alexander's funeral. The war was still active but thankfully John's family was safe, as the fighting had died down considerably in the south. Everyone was hopeful the war would end soon without further loss of life. In fact, life had almost returned to its mundane routine from before the war. Thomas was busy with his law practice in London, Mary and Katherine were running after the children, and John had returned to Virginia.

John arrived in Accomac on a crisp fall day and only planned to stay in town for two weeks to provision his ship. Even though there had been no skirmishes near his family's home, Mary was still nervous about the war following the loss of Uncle Alexander, and John had promised he would return immediately.

He was looking forward to his return to England as his horse crunched through the fallen yellow leaves that covered the road in a blanket of gold. The sun was shining through the thinning branches and the birds were providing him a happy song while he rode out to Henry Pedenden's house.

"Hello, Henry!" John said as he approached Pedenden's barn, waving.

"John! How nice to see you. When did you get back here?" Pedenden shoved his pitchfork into a pile of hay, wiped the sweat from his brow with his forearm, and walked toward John. He removed his leather work gloves.

John climbed down from his horse and reached out to shake Henry's hand. "I got in a few weeks ago and I'm only staying long enough to load my ship. I'm sailing back in the next few days, as soon as my crew is ready to depart. . I came by because Littleton said you had some family members you want me to transport to Virginia. Do you still need me to do that?"

"Yes, yes, I do. It's my brother's family. Do you have room for eleven passengers?"

"For you? Of course. Write down their

names and I'll make sure to find them as soon as I dock in London."

"I don't have money but I can pay you in land. I have five hundred fifty acres in Northampton I can give you for their transport."

"That will be fine, Henry. You know I'll do anything I can to help, especially for my favorite neighbor." John smiled.

"You're in a good mood today."

"Nothing to frown about today. It's a lovely fall day and I'm soon heading home to my family."

Pedenden looked at him oddly. "I wanted to bring my family over last summer, but that was only for their headrights so I could increase the size of my farm. Now it's become a matter of life or death."

"Life or death?"

"Oh, you haven't heard." Pedenden looked down at his dirt-crusted boots and kicked a rock like a schoolboy who didn't want to tell the truth.

"Heard what, Henry?"

Henry looked back up at John and sighed. "There was a battle at Southwell in Nottinghamshire and the king surrendered to the Scots."

"What?"

"Cromwell and Fairfax took the formal surrender of the royalists at Oxford. Royalists are being arrested by Parliament in droves.

That's why I need to get my family out of there."

"What?!" John repeated. He felt as if he would throw up.

"I'm afraid it's true, John. If you have family serving the king, you'd better get them out of there before Cromwell has them hung."

"My brother is a colonel in the king's army. He has my wife and children in his keeping."

Pedenden groaned. "You'd better get back there quickly and figure out how to get them out of the country before Cromwell shuts the whole seaport down. They're already charging some royalists with treason." He leaned closer to John and lowered his voice as if someone was listening. "Some have already been beheaded."

"When did you hear this?" John asked, his chest constricted.

"Just heard it yesterday from Berkeley."

John quickly wrote down the names of Pedenden's family members and hastened back to the dock to finish loading his ship. He kept his men working throughout the night so they could sail at first light. As the first rays of dawn showed their pink and purple fingers across the sky, Berkeley galloped onto the dockyard.

"John, I need to speak with you," Berkeley called.

"I've already heard, Will. I'm leaving immediately." John didn't stop working to greet his friend.

"That's what I came to speak with you about." Berkeley climbed down from his horse. "Pedenden told me you're heading back. You can't just waltz into London on a gigantic ship right now. Parliament is guarding all the waterways and docks. You'll need to find a way to sneak into the country if you want to get to Thomas. And with the chaos in London, I'm afraid you'll never find a way to contact him right now. Certainly he's already in hiding at this point. Royalist armies have been surrendering all over the country. We've lost Newark, Oxford, Exeter, and at least a dozen other garrisons. Worcester and Wallingford Castle surrendered, and I just received word this morning that Raglan Castle in Wales has done the same."

John didn't stop moving. He picked up a large crate and carried it up the tilted gangway. He stopped at the top and turned back to Berkeley. "So, what am I supposed to do? Sit here and wait?"

"It gets worse, John. Cromwell convened Parliament to pass a law to seize all lands and possessions of the royalists. Royalists' property is now to be used for the good of the commonwealth. Your family may not even be at Greenway Court anymore."

John walked back down the gangway and placed the crate on the ground. "My uncle warned me this would happen if Parliament won. So, this is really it? We're finished?"

"I'm afraid so. They're holding the king under guard at Holdenby House. It's over, John."

John remained as still as a statue as he tried to process all that were lost. After a moment, he asked, "How am I going to get my family out?"

"Well, for God's sake, don't sail down the Thames in broad daylight. You don't want Cromwell's men to set their sights on you and your family. I wouldn't be surprised if they fired a cannon on your ship upon your arrival. If they sink it, you won't have any way to get your family out, and if they don't already have Thomas in custody, your presence could seal his fate. They could detain you just to bring him out of hiding."

John picked up the crate and walked back up the gangway.

Berkeley followed him. "John, stop!"

John turned and looked at him. "I have to get to my family, Will."

"You don't even know what you're walking into, and you're not even certain where your family is at this point. Thomas may have taken them into hiding. I'm sure he will send word to you, but you need to remain here and wait for instructions from him. You don't know where to find him, but he knows where to find you."

"I have to get my wife and sons out of England." John sounded like a parrot.

"But you're not going to do that if you don't know where they are. Trust me. Wait for word from Thomas. I know he's never let you down. He won't this time, either."

John stopped in the middle of the gangway. He knew Berkeley was right, but how was he supposed to sit on the shores of Virginia and wait? How long would he have to wonder about the fate of his wife and sons? Was Thomas even free or alive to send word? Had Parliament already seized his family's property?

Berkeley broke his train of thought. "John, trust me. Wait until you receive word from Thomas."

John nodded, then turned and carried the crate onto his ship, leaving Berkeley alone at the foot of the gangplank.

CHAPTER 16

June 3, 1647, Kidnap

"He did what?!" Oliver Cromwell shouted, veins bulging from his temples.

"Fairfax took the king from Holdenby House, sir. He kidnapped him right out from under our guards. He sent this message for you." William Lenthall handed a piece of paper to Cromwell.

Cromwell snatched the paper from Lenthall's hand and unfolded it. A half dozen men stood around him in the near empty chambers of the House of Commons. They remained silent as they watched him read the letter. The brittle paper rattled as Cromwell's hands began to tremble with rage.

Cromwell didn't look up from the paper

as he spoke. "It says the king is now in his custody and any further negotiations will have to be conducted through him. It says the king went willingly and is in good health. I can't believe this!" He flipped the paper over and over. "It doesn't say where he's taken him."

"Why would the king go with him willingly?" Lenthall asked.

Cromwell's face reddened as he crumpled the paper and glared at Lenthall. "Fairfax has been a brazen upstart since the day he was born. In the last five years since he became general, he's done nothing but undermine my every effort to secure this realm. I'm sure he's made it very clear to the king that he has turned against me and is trying to divide our army, and the king probably sees this as an opportunity to divide us further."

"What do you want us to do, sir?" one of the men asked Cromwell.

"I want someone to go to Holdenby House and find out how the hell this happened, and then I want someone to find Fairfax and deliver his head to me on a plate!" Cromwell turned and stormed out of the room, slamming the door behind him.

CHAPTER 17

November 11, 1647, Escape

The king had initially been taken by Fairfax's men to New Market, but after hearing that Cromwell's men were nearing their hiding place, Fairfax ordered the king taken to Oatlands. A month after arriving at Oatlands, Cromwell's men were again on their trail, so the king, under his own recommendation, was moved to Hampton Court.

Just as Cromwell suspected, the king saw his captivity with Fairfax as an opportunity to turn the tide of the war. If Cromwell and Fairfax were at each other's throats, one would have to eventually emerge the victor. When that happened, which one would their treasonous army follow? Perhaps now the king's royal army, which had so willingly abandoned him, would see that only one ruler was best for the kingdom, not the joint venture between Cromwell and Fairfax. Only one ruler could see to it that the country and the army was not divided. While the king bided his time, awaiting the certain collapse of the army that detained him, he knew he still had many supporters at Hampton Court. He requested to be taken there, and after he arrived, he secretly asked his supporters to help him plan a covert escape. He promised them great rewards in return for their loyalty.

Hampton Court was a well-fortified castle from where no prisoner could escape, so Fairfax was confident in moving the king there. He also allowed the king daily walks in the central courtyard, under guard. The king always requested that a host of servant boys accompany him on his strolls and the guards were happy to oblige, cutting down on their monotonous duty of watching the king's every move, every moment of every day.

The king would walk around the courtyard, a handful of young men escorting him, and after an hour or so, the king would return to the guards at the door and request to be taken back to his chambers. It was a mind-numbing routine and the guards became lax in their supervision.

On November 11, after a month of daily

walks, everything changed. The king was in the middle of his routine when a handful of the servant boys erupted into a fistfight in the middle of the courtyard.

"No, I'm the king's favorite!" hollered one boy.

Another punched him in the face. "I am! I walk next to the king."

A third entered the brawl, trying to break up the boys, but he was hit in the jaw by a stray fist and began punching back. Soon a fourth and fifth boy entered the scuffle.

The two guards who had been chatting in the arched doorway of the courtyard ran over to break up the melee. The boys began punching and kicking them.

In the confusion, two servant boys whisked the king away, ushering His Majesty into the doorway and out of harm's way.

The two boys and the king, dressed as beggars, entered the tunnels beneath the castle and escaped from Hampton Court. They then headed south, unrecognized. The journey took them weeks, but when they finally arrived at the shores of the English Channel, the boys stole a boat and sailed the king to the Isle of Wight. The king was confident he would find an ally there in his old friend, Governor Robert Hammond.

The elderly governor, surprised by the king's arrival, greeted him warmly and gave him the best rooms in Carisbrooke Castle. Over a feast of eel and swan, the king proposed his plan to retake the throne and offered Hammond great riches in exchange for his help. At the end of the meal, the king thanked Hammond for his kindness and support.

When night fell, Hammond placed a guard outside the king's door, explaining it was for the king's own safety. He then sent a message to Cromwell, telling him the king was back in Parliament's custody.

The king was outraged that Hammond would turn on him, but unbeknownst to Hammond, Hampton Court was not the only place the king had found supporters. Through loyal servants at Carisbrooke Castle, the king spent the next month in secret negotiations with the Scots, sending and receiving messages through the cook, the stable boy, the boatswain, and one of the chambermaids. By the end of December, under Hammond's very nose, the king had signed a treaty with the Scots, agreeing to establish Presbyterianism in England if they would invade England on his behalf and restore him to his rightful throne.

Word of the treaty spread quickly throughout the royalist armies, and with the help of the Scots, the royalists planned several attacks to take back towns in Kent, Essex, Cumberland, and south Wales.

CHAPTER 18

December 26, 1647, Secret Treaty

John spent two months waiting in Virginia, as Berkeley suggested. But after receiving no word from Thomas, he couldn't take the waiting any longer and sailed back to London. The voyage had the worst weather John and his crew had ever encountered. The mighty ship endured over two months of horrific storms, and when they finally sailed up the Thames, they arrived to the sight of strange soldiers on the London wharf. At first, the soldiers made the crew nervous, but the armed men didn't approach the ship. The crew remained on the ship, quiet and cautious. After two days, John came to the conclusion that the soldiers were just there for looks. He disembarked the vessel and was never stopped or questioned.

He casually strolled through the dockyard and left the area. He walked straight to the livery where he hired a horse. Once he was sure he was out of sight of the soldiers, he rode like lightning to Greenway Court, hoping to find at least a message telling him where his family had been taken. He arrived at the manor house just before nightfall, busted through the front door, and found Thomas sitting at the dining table, drinking a pint of ale as if nothing was happening in the country.

After greeting his wife and children, John sat down with his brother. "Thomas, what is going on here? I heard the king surrendered and I thought you were all dead. I think it's time we get the children out of England."

"The children are fine, John." Thomas leaned forward and lowered his voice. "I spoke with my men at the king's side. Parliament was holding the king, but Fairfax's officers kidnapped him and placed him in protective custody."

"Fairfax now has the king?"

"No, the king is back in Cromwell's custody now."

John stared at Thomas, waiting for him to explain what the hell was going on.

Thomas waved his hand in the air. "Oh,

it's a long story, but what Fairfax accomplished when he kidnapped the king was essentially dividing the parliamentarian army."

"Dividing the army? That doesn't make any sense. Why would Fairfax want to do that? Why would he split off from Parliament?"

"I heard he has had more than enough of Cromwell's tyranny. After Leicester surrendered, Cromwell took Basing House. Three hundred royalists surrendered. Cromwell killed one hundred of them *after* they surrendered."

John's jaw dropped.

Thomas continued. "I think that was the deciding moment for Fairfax, and he soon began distancing himself from Cromwell. Fairfax is a member of the gentry. Our class does not do things like that. Cromwell's actions only show what a lowlife he really is. I also think Fairfax seeks his own fortunes in this war." Thomas took a bite of his bread and followed it with a sip of ale. "I've been in the king's service for some time and I know how he thinks. I know he recognizes the division between Cromwell and Fairfax as an opportunity to divide them further. He went willingly with Fairfax's men when they moved him to Hampton Court, which we all knew was an easy place for him to escape from. It was only a matter of time. After all, he knows every tunnel and door in that palace."

"What happened after he escaped?"

"He made contact with Robert Hammond, the governor of the Isle of Wight, who he thought would be sympathetic, but Hammond turned on him and informed Parliament that he was there. The king found strong supporters in the castle, though. He got word to the Scots and promised to establish Presbyterianism in England if they would invade the country on his behalf."

"They believed him and agreed to do that?"

"They are raising an army even as we speak and are planning a massive invasion."

"So, our family is safe?"

Thomas nodded. "That's why we always side with the king, little brother." He patted John on the shoulder.

John took a deep breath and exhaled, feeling as if he could breathe for the first time in months. In his head, he replayed conversations with his uncle and with Berkeley. "What about Parliament's threat to seize our property?"

"They haven't come near Greenway Court. They've been showing a little muscle toward some of the royalists in the north, but they're too busy arguing over who's running the army and the future of the country. I'm sure they don't know anything of the treaty with the Scots. The king is at Carisbrooke Castle, keeping them busy asking for negotiations. Parliament voted in favor of negotiations, but Cromwell said King

Charles is a bloody tyrant and claimed he will arrest anyone who comes to the negotiation table, so most of Parliament is staying away from London. They're afraid of Fairfax's army and even more frightened of Cromwell's temper. Cromwell is pushing to run the country himself and is halting every proposition Parliament is presenting. Cromwell wants the country to become the English Commonwealth under his own rule, but Parliament doesn't know what it wants. I'll tell you one thing, Cromwell is splitting Parliament right down the middle as effectively as Fairfax split the army. Oliver Cromwell is no king and never will be."

"So, the royalists are rising up with the Scots?"

"Yes, indeed. Many right here in Kent and in Essex. George Goring has raised ten thousand men. We're holding Gravesend, Rochester, Dover, and Maidstone."

"I thought the war was over once the king was captured," John said.

"Most definitely not, little brother. This coming battle, with the help of the Scots, shall be the end of the war. We shall be victorious and we'll shortly place Charles back on the throne. That will be the end of the war. We shall soon see Cromwell's head on the executioner's block and I can't wait for that day."

CHAPTER 19

June 1648, Battle at Maidstone

After being assured of his family's safety, John sailed back to Virginia to resume his business. As usual, he left his wife and children in the capable hands of his brother.

On a cloudy, storm-threatening morning, Thomas rose from the breakfast table and kissed his wife on the top of her head. "Good-bye, my dear. I'll be seeing to the king's business today. I am joining George Goring and moving two thousand men here to Maidstone."

"Is there to be a battle here?" Katherine asked. She wrung her hands together and her eyes became large with worry.

"There's word that Fairfax is moving his

army this way, but no, I don't think there will be any battles here. Fairfax is just showing his muscle, and we're simply moving the men here to guard the town."

"Be careful, my dear," Katherine said as she rose to walk him to the door.

"I'll be fine. You keep the children within arm's reach today just in case."

"In case what?"

"In case Fairfax decides to flex that muscle and two thousand men aren't enough."

Katherine stood in the doorway, listening to the thunder rumbling in the distance, and watched her husband gallop toward the road. When he was out of sight, she looked up at the sky. Dark thunderheads were forming. The air smelled humid. There would be great storms today, of that she had no doubt. She prayed for Thomas's safety and for his quick return.

* * *

The Scots had done as promised and invaded England at the king's request. The spring had seen skirmish after skirmish with royalist and Scottish uprisings throughout England. The parliamentarians had their hands full as the massive Scottish invasion occurred from the north at the same time as a rebellion arose in Wales. Parliamentary forces were spread thin and most of Cromwell's men were in the north, fighting in Wales. Fairfax and his diminished army of six thousand maintained control of London and most of the surrounding towns. They had squashed most of the uprisings, but Goring, Culpepper, and others, holding many towns in Kent, Essex, and Sussex, showed amazing resilience and stamina. The battles to the south of London became prolonged as the gentry refused to surrender to Parliament. They made it abundantly clear they were in the service of the king and would never surrender, as many in the north had done.

Thomas rode to Penenden Heath, outside of Maidstone, and joined forces with his friend George Goring and his ten thousand men, who had been assembled in anticipation of Fairfax's advance. They divided the men and sent each division to protect the surrounding towns. While some stayed in Penenden Heath with Goring, some moved to Burham Heath, some went to Aylesford, and two thousand men moved to Maidstone with Thomas.

On June 1, Fairfax's army arrived in Burham Heath and the royalists wasted no time in engaging them. The skirmish ended badly for the royalists and Fairfax took the town. He continued his march southward and took Penenden Heath, decimating Goring's army.

Thomas was in the process of moving his two thousand men to Maidstone when Fairfax's army crossed the River Medway and the East

Farleigh Bridge, effectively dividing Thomas's army in half, leaving half in Aylesford and half approaching Maidstone.

When the afternoon grew late, the heavens opened up and heavy rains fell on Maidstone, but that did not stop Fairfax's advance. His troops attacked Thomas's army from behind. Their powder had become wet in the storm so they couldn't use their muskets, but they fought with their longbows and swords. Fairfax's men pushed Thomas's soldiers back street by street, inch by inch. Lightning flashed as the royalists fought near Gabriel's Hill. Thunder pounded their ears as they were moved back further to Week Street.

By the time evening turned to night, Thomas and his men had been pushed back to St. Faith's Churchyard. They fought among massive oaks and tombstones, often not knowing which sounds were thunder and which were cannon fire. Thomas's men held their ground.

As midnight fell, the fighting died down and Thomas's men found shelter inside the church. The thunderstorm had flooded the cemetery and the torrents had seeped under the door of the church, covering the floor in inches of rainwater. The soldiers lay on the pews, wondering what they would do come morning. They were tired. They were cold and wet. They didn't know how they would escape from the church that had now become a prison since Fairfax's army had the building surrounded. What was left of their ammunition was wet and useless.

In the wee hours of the morning, the storms subsided, and the two armies sat in silence until the night gave way to the soft light of early morning. Thomas looked out the window and saw Fairfax, dressed in black, gallop onto the scene on his white horse. The man spoke to his commander, and though Thomas couldn't make out their words, he could tell by Fairfax's gestures that he was instructing the man to allow the royalist soldiers to emerge from the church and then the commander should send them home.

Thomas understood the move. Fairfax only wanted to capture the town; he didn't want to be responsible for a thousand prisoners. Thomas instructed his men to wave a white flag and surrender. He needed them to stay alive to fight another day. Staying holed up in this church with no ammunition would not win the war. They had to keep their eyes on the larger prize.

One of the men cracked open the church door and stuck a white cloth through the opening, waving it at Fairfax's man. Slowly, the soldiers exited, arms behind their heads.

Fairfax had won Maidstone.

Since St. Faith's Church was flooded, the

prisoners, under the shadow of muskets and swords, were commanded to walk single file up the hill to All Saints Church, where Fairfax's men would catalog their names and release them, making them promise to lay down their arms and return home.

Thomas stayed with his men but remained silent at the back of the line, his head bowed, his eyes meeting no one's. At All Saints Church, Thomas stood in the kaleidoscope of sunny colors blazing through the stained-glass windows and gazed down at his uncle Alexander's tomb. He was certain his men had fought a brave battle, but as he stared at the tomb, he wondered if he could have done more. His men were before him, lined up like cattle ready to go to slaughter. He felt their fate was even worse than death, for they were giving up their pride and their king.

Perhaps he was being hard on himself. Perhaps he was just tired. After all, he had not felt the comfort of a soft bed for the last forty-eight hours.

After staring at the tomb for more than an hour and listening to his soldier's names being taken at the front of the line, Thomas decided to follow in his uncle's footsteps. They could take his name on this day. They could take his arms and his horse. They could disband his men, but they would never take his spirit nor his ambition to see the king back on the throne. He would live to see these men with their ink pots and quills beheaded for treason. He would fight for his king until his final breath. Today was not the end. In fact, today was a new beginning.

When he was the only soldier left in the church, he raised his head and stepped away from his uncle's tomb. He marched to the table set up near the door and looked down at the soldier sitting behind it. He found himself gazing into the eyes of General Thomas Fairfax.

"Well, Colonel Thomas Culpepper, do you claim command of these men?"

"No, these are George Goring's men. I am only here to serve."

"Goring? That traitor? It seems you have chosen to serve the wrong side."

"When all is said and done, we'll see if that is true, but I suspect you're mistaken."

Fairfax sighed and scribbled Thomas's name on the paper in front of him. He spoke without looking up at Thomas. "Colonel Culpepper, in exchange for your freedom on this day, you are to lay down your arms and return to your home. Do you understand?"

"I understand," Thomas lied without a flinch.

"Then you are free to go," Fairfax said.

Thomas didn't move.

Fairfax looked up.

Thomas said, "I hope you know what you're doing, Thomas Fairfax. It will be a great shame when we change places and you're forced to give up your talents as a competent military leader, only to find your head on a spike next to Cromwell's."

Fairfax narrowed his eyes. "Is that a threat, Culpepper?"

"No, just an observation."

A bead of sweat appeared on the general's forehead. He looked around at his own men loitering in the church. "We are finished here."

CHAPTER 20

July 1648, Siege of Colchester

When the war began six years earlier, George Goring had been sent from the country to garner support for the king. He traveled to Paris and met with Cardinal Mazarin, requesting arms and money to support England. After the meeting ended successfully, he sent word of his accomplishment to the queen in the Netherlands, but somehow Parliament intercepted his letter. He was charged with treason, his property and manors seized, his family scattered. Since his stately manor was now in the hands of Parliament, his two sons were exiled to France while his daughters and his wife moved in with her family in Colchester.

For his own safety, Goring remained abroad in France and Denmark until he was called by the king to take back Taunton. After failing to accomplish this task, then losing Bridgewater and now Maidstone, he knew the only way to win the war was to take London. He rallied nearly six thousand royalists from Kent and the surrounding areas and moved north. The army that controlled London controlled everything.

Thomas rode his horse next to Goring's, not bothering to make small talk. Both men knew what needed to be done. It wouldn't be an easy battle, but no battle worth fighting ever was. Thomas heard a galloping horse approaching from behind, and he turned to see a young messenger ride up to Goring, waving a piece of paper.

Goring stopped his horse and took the letter. As he read, a great worry crossed the sixty-year-old man's weathered face. "We have to move quickly," Goring said, still looking at the paper.

"What happened?" Thomas asked.

"Fairfax has gotten word of our advance and is in pursuit."

Thomas felt adrenaline in his veins and dread in his gut. Why did Fairfax always know where they were and what they were doing? Even if they managed to take London, Fairfax would be at their backs and they would be surrounded.

Goring kicked his horse in the ribs and galloped toward the men in front of them. Thomas knew Goring was telling them to speed up, but the slow-moving artillery behind them couldn't go much faster. The horses were exhausted and so were the men. For the rest of the day, they somehow managed to stay ahead of Fairfax, but when they arrived in London in the late afternoon, they found the city's gates closed. There would be no attack if they couldn't get into the city.

"We'll have to continue forward," Goring said.

"Where to?" Thomas asked.

"Colchester."

As the evening sky turned to black, they continued east, crossing the Thames, and marching into Essex with Fairfax's men close behind. They made their way sixty miles to Colchester—Goring's hometown—where they entered the town's gates. Fairfax's army wasn't anywhere to be seen. A young messenger reported that Fairfax had stopped his army for the night. Goring's men sealed the town's gates and posted sentries at every vantage point.

Goring took Thomas to the home where his wife and daughters were staying.

"Thomas, I'd like you to meet my wife, Lady Mary Goring, and my daughters, Elizabeth and Catherine."

Thomas greeted the ladies and shared a

bowl of porridge with them. Goring filled his wife in on the recent battles. She seemed relieved he was home safe, until he mentioned that Fairfax's army was tailing them and would probably be at the town's gates at first light. Thomas saw Lady Mary's face fill with fear and imagined his wife would react the same way.

"Don't worry, my dear, our town is well fortified. We have abundant ammunition and six thousand soldiers. We'll take Fairfax down right here, then we will find a way to take London," Goring said to his wife.

Thomas wasn't so sure. How would they take London? The gates were never open anymore.

Lady Mary said, "George, I'm sure your army is up to the challenge, but we don't have enough food in the town to feed six thousand men."

"We'll be fine."

* * *

The next morning, Fairfax's army surrounded the town. The fighting began in earnest, but Goring's men held Fairfax at bay for the first week. On the eighth day, cannon fire rained down upon the town and over one thousand of Goring's men were killed. Lady Mary Goring, who had suffered through so much with her sons exiled and her husband off fighting for the king, was also killed. Thomas thought Goring might falter in his command after the loss of his wife, but her death only made Goring more determined to conquer Fairfax and the entire parliamentarian army.

They fought well for another few weeks, and though they had plenty of munitions, as Lady Mary had said, they didn't have enough food to remain pinned down for an indefinite length of time. After eleven weeks of fighting, near-starvation finally brought the royalist army out of Colchester. In late August, they surrendered to Fairfax.

Tired and hungry, Thomas observed the events from his knees, his arms bound behind his back. He watched in horror as his comrades, Sir Charles Lucas and Sir George Lisle, were executed on the spot. At the far end of the road, Thomas saw Goring being thrown into the back of a mule-pulled cart, his mouth gagged, his hands tied. Fairfax shouted to his men to "take the traitor to the tower," then climbed onto his white stallion and galloped away. At least Thomas wouldn't have to face Fairfax today.

Thomas was marched with his army to the tower in London, and within weeks, he was brought in front of Parliament to answer to charges. Neither Cromwell nor Fairfax were in attendance, and the men running the trial didn't recognize Thomas as one who had previously vowed to lay down his arms. Therefore, being a member of the gentry class, he was allowed to ransom his freedom with a sizable amount of money. He walked out of the House of Commons a free man, but a destitute one. Only Greenway Court and his son's home of Leeds Castle were left, but at least he had his freedom, which was more than George Goring had.

Goring, having been previously charged with treason, was held in the tower, where he would remain until Parliament decided what to do with him. Thomas knew if Parliament won the war, Goring would face beheading.

Worn and weary from more than three months of fighting on little sleep and less food, Thomas began walking home. His mind spun with horrible scenarios of his country's future. He worried about his soldiers and his friend George, but his mind was mostly occupied with getting home to his wife. He had been gone since June and she probably thought him long dead by now. He walked all the way from London to Greenway Court. It took him nearly two days.

CHAPTER 21

September 1648, Refuge at Leeds Castle

Mary was picking the last of the vegetables from the fall garden and saw him first. "Katherine! Katherine! It's Thomas! He's home!"

Katherine emerged from around the corner of the house and saw her husband walking up the road. He was thin and weary, but he was home! She ran to him and wrapped her arms around his neck. "I thought you dead, my love."

"I am not dead, my dear wife, but I feel I may be soon if I don't sit down and get some food in my belly."

She escorted him inside, barraging him with a million questions about his experiences and whereabouts for the last four months. As she settled him into a chair at the dining table, she instructed the kitchen girl to make him some food and heat a tub of water for him to bathe. He ate like she had never seen him eat before. She let him finish eating before she spoke. "Thomas, I'm so relieved you're home and safe."

"Well, I'm home, but I don't know how safe we are."

She escorted him to the bathhouse, removed his soiled clothes, and bathed and shaved him while he told her the horrific tale of his capture. "I'm afraid I've spent all our fortunes securing my release from Fairfax. I don't know what we're going to do now. All we have left is Greenway Court, and if we can't return the king to the throne, we may lose that to Cromwell. I want you to take the children and go into hiding at Leeds Castle. You and Mary and the children need to move into the cellar for your own safety. If Cromwell or Fairfax come looking for me, it will be too dangerous for you here. I swore an oath to Fairfax to lay down my arms, and since I was captured at Colchester, I'm now in great risk of being arrested for treason."

"This doesn't make any sense. How can Cromwell and Fairfax turn so quickly against the monarch who has made this country so great?"

"My dear, the king is not in power

anymore. Cromwell is holding him. They moved him to Hurst Castle, and I don't know what they're going to do with him but I suspect the worst."

"They wouldn't do anything to the king, would they?"

"These men are determined to rule the country. The only way they can do that is to do away with the king. Even more dangerous is that Cromwell and Fairfax are at each other's throats. If they dispose of the king, I don't know that the war will end there. They will probably continue the war, fighting each other."

Tears welled up in Katherine's eyes and a small sob escaped. She placed her fingers to her lips in an attempt to keep herself from crying.

Thomas looked at her with a compassion she seldom witnessed. He was always in complete control, but at this moment, he looked as if he would cry with her.

"I'll tell Mary to pack her children, and we'll all go to Leeds as you've directed."

He reached for her hand and water dripped onto her blue dress, causing dark spots as it soaked into the satin. "You'll be safe there, I promise."

"What about you?"

"I need to go to Southampton tomorrow. JC sent word for me to meet him there. He has men inside Hurst Castle who can get him in to speak with the king. He thinks the only thing we can do at this point to save the king's life is to negotiate, so he's going to convince the king to allow him to do so. We'll then go to London and if he can convince Cromwell to accept the king's terms, perhaps this will all be over soon. If not, I'm afraid this will not end well for the king. In all probability, it won't end well for any of us. Either way, I want you and the children safe at Leeds Castle. I'll send word to John to come to your aid. When he arrives, you go with him without delay. I'll be near, but I'm certainly not going to wait here for Fairfax to show up and arrest me." He looked into her eyes. "I'll be watching over you, and I will be with you again. I promise."

CHAPTER 22

November 1648, Negotiations

"Gentlemen, I appear before you on behalf of His Majesty, King Charles," JC said as he stood in front of his former colleagues at the House of Commons.

"What do you mean, on behalf of the king?" Cromwell asked.

"I have been given sole authority to negotiate on the king's behalf, given to me directly from His Majesty."

"When exactly did you speak with the king?" Cromwell demanded.

"I'm afraid I'm not at liberty to give you that information, but I am here as a representative of His Majesty to negotiate a settlement with Parliament and bring an end to this war. His Majesty has instructed me to offer each of you amnesty for your treasonous actions. You will avoid all charges of betrayal and disloyalty and subsequent beheadings if you immediately replace the king to his rightful throne. I am also instructed to warn you that His Majesty's armies are again assembling, and you will soon find yourselves in dire circumstances if you continue your current course." JC tucked his hand in his pocket and awaited a response.

Cromwell rose to his feet. "Lord Culpepper, we are not the least bit interested in negotiating with you. How do we even know you're telling the truth?"

"The king anticipated your skepticism." JC unfolded a piece of paper with the king's signature that instructs the House of Commons to follow the initiative JC offered. Cromwell frowned and passed the paper to the man nearest him. As the paper made its way around the table, the din grew louder. Cromwell slammed his fist on the table in front of him. Everyone silenced and watched him rise from his chair and walk around the table. He moved stiffly, as though his legs ached. His nearly fifty years were beginning to show in his graying hair, but his eyes held a hatred that wasn't there only six years earlier.

"Lord Culpepper, I don't know what kind of game you're playing here, but as I previously stated, we are not the least bit interested in negotiating with you or with that tyrant you refer to as king. As a matter of fact, most of us agree you should be locked in the tower immediately. If you don't have anything further to add, you should avail yourself of the nearest exit as quickly as possible." His voice rose with each passing word, and by the time he reached JC, spittle was flying from his lips as he spoke.

JC backed up a few feet and looked around the room at the men he once called comrades. Some had even been friends. "I'm deeply saddened for you and I'm sorry it has come to this, gentlemen. I hope you all know what you're doing. It will be with great sorrow that I witness your executions." He turned and marched past the sergeant at arms through the massive arched doorway. The room erupted into a caterwauling of shouts and comments, each man trying to speak over the other. The speaker of the House pounded his gavel on the desk, trying to restore order.

* * *

Thomas accompanied JC to the dock, where JC was to board a waiting vessel bound for Denmark. He was prepared for the negotiations to end badly.

"Even a blind man can see this war isn't going to end well for the king," JC said.

"Well, you need to be at the prince's side," Thomas said.

"Yes, I shall return to the prince at once." He shook his head. "I can't believe the leaders of the House of Commons are not even modestly flexible, and the ones who could be persuaded to negotiate with the king don't have the courage to raise their objections before Oliver Cromwell."

"They know they'll face arrest and execution if they rise against Cromwell at this point."

"Especially now that Cromwell holds the king in custody and is so close to winning the war," JC said.

"Cousin, you have only one important job in the world now—to protect Prince Charles. You can't do anything else for the king."

JC nodded, knowing Thomas was right. He would take the prince to his mother in France, where the future king of England would be safe. When that young man ascended to the throne someday, JC would happily see Cromwell's head on a spike.

"What are you going to do now?" JC asked.

"I'm going to stay in hiding at Goring's son's barn until I can get word to John. Parliament seized the property months ago but they never come near it so I'm safe for now."

"Stay safe, cousin. I'll be in Demark or

France or somewhere."

The two quickly hugged each other good-bye. Thomas watched JC board the ship but didn't wait for it to sail. He rode off on his horse, leaving a trail of dust in his wake.

* * *

Back at the House of Commons, Cromwell demanded the king be immediately moved from Hurst Castle to Windsor Castle, which he thought would be more secure. "Let's see if anyone else can speak to the king without my consent."

For the next week, Parliament debated whether or not to negotiate with the king and put an end to the war. Many abstained from the vote, but one hundred twenty-nine members voted in favor of negotiation. Eighty-three opposed. Cromwell was one of those in opposition.

"How can you men even consider negotiating with someone who has ruled as a tyrant? He has reigned with ruthless intent and declared war upon Parliament and his own people," Cromwell roared before the members of the House.

Many mumbled in agreement, others sat in silence wondering why there was still discussion when the vote had been cast. When the meeting was adjourned and the men had left the room, Cromwell called for the sergeant at arms and ordered the arrest of every member who voted in favor of the negotiations.

At the next session of Parliament, forty-five members were arrested upon their arrival and another one hundred eighty-six were turned away at the door for being supporters of the king. The action caused an uproar unlike the House of Commons had ever seen, and another eighty-six members left the session in protest. Cromwell was left with only two hundred men to create a list of charges against the king. Within a few days, the House of Commons penned the accusations and charged the king with treason.

Cromwell sent a copy of the charges to the House of Lords, which unanimously rejected the charges. The following morning, the chief justices of the three common-law courts declared the indictment unlawful.

Cromwell took the floor without the speaker giving it to him. No one in the chamber objected.

"We will not allow the lords and the justices to get away with this. We've been at the mercy of this dictator for over two decades. He has ruled with malice and wickedness, illegally taxing his people, imprisoning them, executing them. We now have him in our custody and we will not let this opportunity slip by. We shall rise to the occasion. We shall stand bravely and take responsibility for our future and our country, even for the spineless members of the House of Lords and the chief justice, our own countrymen, who obviously have no courage or backbone to stand up to this oppressive and totalitarian king."

The remaining members of the House of Commons roared in approval, and so going against the House of Lords and the chief justices, the House of Commons, under the direction of Oliver Cromwell, declared itself capable of legislating alone and created a separate court for the king's trial. Members elected a High Court of Justice with three judges and one hundred thirty-five commissioners, many of whom refused to participate in the proceedings.

The first day of the trial, which was held at Westminster Hall, saw only sixty-eight of those elected in attendance. General Thomas Fairfax was one of them. He and Oliver Cromwell sneered at each other from across the room.

CHAPTER 23

January 20, 1649, Trial

The high court of sixty-eight commissioners sat in Westminster Hall and awaited the arrival of the king. Between the damp and clammy weather and the nervous tension in the room, the air was palpable. A majority of the commissioners and none of the citizens in the gallery had seen the king for the last seven years, and there was a collective gasp at first sight of him. The sergeant at arms escorted the graying and thin monarch and offered him a seat in the middle of the room, right in front of the president of the court's desk. The king moved slowly as if in pain, and he held on to both arms of the chair as he lowered himself into it.

Whispers silenced as the solicitor general John Cook, who was the acting prosecutor for the trial, walked to the center of the room. He was visibly nervous, his face pale and his hands trembling. He tucked one hand into his pocket and formed a fist with the other to hide his anxiety. Everyone in the room knew if this didn't go well, all sixty-eight members would find their heads on stakes around London. If it did go well, they still may find themselves in dire circumstance. It was not every day a high court was elected to try a king for treason.

John Cook cleared his throat and opened his mouth to say something, but he stopped and looked around the room as if he had forgotten why he was there. He cleared his throat again and announced, "His Royal Majesty Charles Stuart, by the grace of God, King of England, Scotland, France, and Ireland." He paused again, finding it difficult to look the king in the eye. He glanced at the floor and back up at the wall behind the gallery of people sitting behind the king. "You are hereby charged with multiple counts of high treason, including whereas you have traitorously and maliciously levied war against Parliament and the people they represent. How do you plead?"

The room was soundless as the king looked from face to face on either side of him. Rows of Parliament's members stared back at him, many with faces the color of white sheets. Most would not meet his eye, but Cromwell glared at him.

After an uncomfortable silence, the king raised his chin and answered. "I would know by what power I am called hither, by what authority? No court has jurisdiction over the monarch. I rule under only one authority, and that is God. No earthly power can justly call me into question. This day's proceedings are not warranted by God's law, for the authority of a king is clearly justified in both the Old and New Testament."

After a moment of chatter from the court and the gallery, the nervous prosecutor raised his voice and repeated the charges, again requesting a plea.

The king answered the same.

The prosecutor repeated the charges a third time.

Before he had a chance to request a plea, the king interrupted him, saying again, "I would know by what power I am called…"

The courtroom erupted in shouts, drowning out the king's repetitive speech. The prosecutor looked at the president of the court and raised his eyebrows, not knowing how to proceed. The president of the court, John Bradshaw, nodded and the prosecutor walked back to his seat, his face red with embarrassment. Bradshaw took over the proceedings and repeatedly pounded his gavel on the wooden desk, attempting to bring the court to order. It was not an easy task, as everyone in the room was emotionally charged. He pounded his gavel for at least five minutes.

When the room was finally silent, Bradshaw spoke to the king. "Your Majesty, you are being charged with treason, with or without a plea. The prosecutor will present a case against you that will prove that you have committed treason against your people and your country."

Over the first three days of the trial, various members of the high court asked the king questions, but the only response they received was the same one questioning the power and authority of the court.

At the end of the third day, tiring of the same response, the commissioners had the king removed from the proceedings, after which the high court heard more than thirty witnesses speak against him.

On January 26, 1649, the court concluded with a vote, finding the king guilty as charged.

The following day, they paraded the king before a public session. The hall was filled to capacity and though the air outside was cool, the inside of Westminster Hall was humid and stifling. The stench of body odor, with an undercurrent of metallic-smelling ink and paper, rose to greet each attendee. Bradshaw pounded his gavel and called the meeting to order.

"We all know why we are here so I will forego an opening statement." He faced the king. "His Royal Majesty Charles Stuart, by the grace of God, King of England, Scotland, France, and Ireland, you have been found guilty on all counts." He turned to the commissioners. "I will read the names of each high court commissioner and request he step forward to add his signature and wax seal to the king's death warrant."

The third to sign was Oliver Cromwell. After adding his wax seal to his signature, he turned and sneered at the king. The king stared back at Cromwell with no expression.

Nearing the end of the roll call, most of the commissioners had signed. Only a handful had refused to do so.

Bradshaw was coming to the last few names on the register. "General Thomas Fairfax."

Silence.

"General Thomas Fairfax," he repeated, louder.

A lady in the gallery stood and said, "If it pleases the court, Lord Fairfax is not in attendance. He sends word that the house has done wrong to name him a commissioner, and that he would never sit among the body and sentence the king to death."

"What is your name, madam?" Bradshaw asked.

"Mr. President, I am Lady Anne Fairfax,

wife of Lord Thomas Fairfax."

A mumble from the gallery arose. Realizing there was nothing he could do about Fairfax's absence, Bradshaw slapped his gavel and continued calling the last of the names.

When all was finished, fifty-nine of the sixty-eight commissioners had added their signatures and wax seals to the king's death warrant. The document looked like a child's drawing of red poppies growing in rows and columns across the paper.

The process had taken more than three hours, and anticipation of the verdict hung over the crowd like an impending thunderstorm. In three hours, no one had moved or said a word. The verdict would be the most astounding the country had ever seen.

After staring at the signatures for a few moments, Bradshaw said, "Your Majesty, would you please rise for the reading of the verdict?"

The king slowly rose from his chair, and Bradshaw handed the piece of paper to the clerk. The only sounds in the hall were the rustle of the paper and the clicks of the clerk's heels on the floor. He stopped in the middle of the room, standing directly before the king, and stared down at the piece of paper that was shaking in his hands.

The king did not look at the paper. He looked into the face of the clerk.

"Your Majesty King Charles, you have

been tried for high treason and crimes against your people. The verdict reads guilty. As punishment for the crime of high treason, you shall be executed by beheading." The clerk bowed his head.

The courtroom broke into shouts, cheers, sobs. No matter how bad the king's crimes, no one in the room thought these men would actually kill their king.

The king stood solemnly in the middle of the pandemonium like a giant tree in the eye of a storm. His expression did not change. He was worn and tired, as the years of war had taken their toll on his health and fortitude. His shoulders slumped slightly but more out of relief that the battle was over, not out of sorrow for the verdict. He stared at the clerk who remained unmoving before him, holding the death warrant in his hands. Four guards appeared around the king, took him by the arms, and escorted him out the back door. The crowd was still screaming as the door slammed closed.

CHAPTER 24

January 30, 1649, Execution

The king was moved to St. James's Palace, where he sat alone for three days. He was placed in a stark, empty room with only a cot and a thin blanket for comfort. The only visitors he was allowed were his two children, Elizabeth and Henry, who were the only members of the royal family still in the country. He asked his daughter to bring him a second shirt, explaining he would wear two shirts on the day of his execution. The weather would be cool this time of year and he didn't want anyone to mistake a shiver for fear. She returned the morning of the execution with a clean and pressed white shirt. He kissed her tenderly on the cheek and wiped her tears away.

She was immediately escorted by guards from the room. No one else came. No one dared get on the wrong side of Parliament. If that group of men could blatantly kill the king, imagine what they could do to anyone else.

At two p.m. on a dreary, foggy afternoon, the king walked slowly under guard from St. James's Palace to Whitehall. Clouds hung low, hiding any warmth the sun might offer. He finally reached the banqueting house where an execution scaffold had been erected. Charles Stuart did not hesitate as he approached it. He climbed up the steps, stopped behind the stone block, looked down at it for a moment, then looked at his citizens. He muttered some words to the enormous group of spectators, who remained barricaded behind soldiers standing shoulder to shoulder. He said a prayer, knelt down, and placed his head on the block. After a moment, he thrust his arms out straight to his sides, and in one clean stroke, he was beheaded.

A collective moan rose from the spectators, followed by tears and cheers. The soldiers parted and allowed people to move forward to get a closer look. Some women dabbed their handkerchiefs in the king's blood, perhaps in sorrow, perhaps as a memento.

A black crow cawed overhead as General Thomas Fairfax, with a cape and hood hiding his identity, turned and walked away from the rear of the crowd.

* * *

Immediately following the king's execution, many homes of the gentry in Kent, Sussex, and Essex were raided. Earls and barons who had supported the king, especially south of London where the resistance was strongest, were rounded up by parliamentary forces. Some were sent to the tower to await trial, some were beheaded, and some were hung on the spot. Many of the ones who made it to trial attempted to buy their way out of the sentencing, but after their property had been seized by Cromwell's men, most didn't have suitable means to purchase their freedom. Following their executions, their families were left to find another, lowlier way to live.

CHAPTER 25

February 5, 1649, Scotland's Proclamation

In Accomac, Virginia, John received word of the king's gruesome demise and wanted desperately to sail to London, but he knew his brother would be in hiding, and the best way to make contact was to wait for word. It pained him to wonder about the fate of his wife and children, but he knew there was nothing he could do until Thomas contacted him. In the words of Berkeley, one couldn't just waltz into London on a big ship. The attention he'd receive would surely end his brother's life.

John also heard that Scotland's Parliament proclaimed the young prince to be

Charles Stuart the Second, King of Great Britain, France, and Ireland, but he knew JC still had the prince in safekeeping in France as the English Parliament denied the proclamation. They declared Scotland's proclamation unlawful, and under the direction and influence of Oliver Cromwell, the English Parliament declared the country to now be the English Commonwealth under the rule of Parliament, not a king.

John wasn't surprised by the news. He knew Cromwell was power hungry and would not allow anyone to rule the country but himself. John received no word of Lord Thomas Fairfax and wondered about the fate of the great general.

Sitting at his kitchen table in his modest two-room shack, John buried his head in his hands. How had his country become such a disaster? He wondered what his father would say about all of this. All those years his father spent coaxing him to be a lawyer was wasted time. A law degree would not help his family now. The only way to save his loved ones was to get them out of the country. He was about to prove his father wrong about owning a ship. His ship would save the Culpeppers from certain destruction. Would his father finally be proud of him? Would his father finally congratulate him on being a good man and a good sailor? His father's scowl passed before John's eyes and he shook his head to make the memory disappear.

He loudly slapped his hands on the table and rose from his chair, almost sending the table toppling backward.

He would sail as soon as he received word from Thomas. His family's lives depended on it.

CHAPTER 26

March 1649, Greenway Court

George Goring had sat in the tower for over seven months since his arrest at Colchester, and in March he was finally brought in front of Parliament to stand trial. Not surprisingly, he was found guilty of treason and his sentence was beheading. His daughters petitioned the court for leniency and a vote was brought in front of the House of Commons. At the end of the vote, the tally was even. A deciding vote needed to be cast by Speaker of the House William Lenthall. The speaker voted *not guilty* and Goring was released to his daughters.

Thomas had been hiding out in Kent at Goring's son's house since he sent his family into hiding at Leeds Castle. He tried repeatedly to get word to John, most days dressing as a beggar and sneaking down to the dockyard, searching for a ship that was sailing to Virginia, but it seemed at every turn, at every dock, he ran into Fairfax's men. They would recognize him instantly, so he would flee and return to his hiding place.

When Thomas heard Goring had been released, he traveled to Colchester under the cloak of darkness to plead with Goring to help him get word to John. But when he arrived, he was informed that Goring had fled the country, traveling to France to help guard the queen and the prince. Goring's daughter Elizabeth agreed to help Thomas, and she finally got a message into a Virginia-bound sailor's hand.

Dear John,

I beseech you to come post haste and see to our wives and children. I have secured them in the hidden cellar rooms at our uncle's house and told them to await your arrival. I fear for their safety and for my own. Brother, when you come, I will be watching from a distance. I shall follow you to your ship and promise to be there before you sail.

Please hurry.

Thomas remained in hiding for months,

riding back and forth between Greenway Court and Leeds Castle. He hid in the trees and thickets and watched for his family, but they never came out. He prayed they were all right. They had been locked up tight for months. He hid the same way at Greenway Court, waiting for Cromwell's soldiers to arrive and destroy his home.

The days and weeks crawled by at a snail's pace as Thomas awaited John's arrival. He found some perverse delight in the fact that their father had always rejected John's idea of owning a ship, and now that very ship would be the lifeline that saved the family. Thomas knew John would arrive soon. He only hoped it would be while the family was still safe and he still had his freedom.

He thought of his friend George Goring. No ship would come to save Goring, but somehow Goring got his life back. Thomas was happy for him. It was a better fate than that of those who were brought to court on the same day Goring was. Four others—the duke of Hamilton, Lord Capel, the earl of Holland, and Sir John Owen—were all found guilty of treason and each received a sentence of death. In the larger picture, Thomas and Goring got off easy, and thanks to Goring's family, Thomas at least had a roof over his head. Daily he ventured down to the docks to check for sightings of his brother. Nightly he rode to Leeds Castle to keep an eye on his family and to Greenway Court to watch over his home. Occasionally he slept.

He knew Parliament would seize Greenway Court eventually. Parliament would eventually take all of the Culpepper properties, but at least the soldiers couldn't get into Leeds Castle unless they wanted to swim the mote, and his son Alex was the official owner of the castle. Parliament couldn't seize it from a minor, unless of course its members rewrote the laws to their benefit, which wouldn't surprise Thomas.

For now, Leeds Castle would remain in his son's possession, at least as long as Thomas was alive. If something happened to Thomas, the property would resort to JC. Thomas didn't understand why Uncle Alexander had included those provisions in his will, but it didn't matter. Thomas was only forty-eight years old. As long as he stayed out of sight, he would be around for a long, long time. Then again, his family probably wouldn't be living in England for much longer, so who cared what happened to the old castle? As long as he got his family safely out of the country, Cromwell could have it.

As the sun rose on a cool April morn, Thomas sat in the woods and watched soldiers invade Greenway Court. They broke down the front door and entered the house, searching for its residents. He narrowed his eyes as he watched them. How dare they enter his home! It was all he could do to remain still and silent as rage boiled in his veins.

They brought household items out of the house one at a time. Furniture, clothing, books. Thomas watched as his wife's treasured platters and silver candlesticks were tossed into the back of a wagon. Across the yard, soldiers had started a fire and items that didn't end up in one of the three wagons were thrown into the growing fire. The paintings of family members that had adorned the dining room walls were pitched like rubbish onto the growing fire. Thomas felt a mixture of sadness and anger, not knowing which was worse. He knew Katherine would be devastated at the loss of such irreplaceable and priceless items. The fire raged higher as more and more items were nonchalantly tossed onto it. The black smoke rose into the air like a snake with no breeze to disperse it, and the crackling of burning wooden objects was only drowned out by the laughter of the soldiers. Thomas clenched his fists in rage and willed himself to remain frozen. He would be no match for the dozen armed men in front of him.

Once the soldiers cleared the house, they went to the stables, knocked the young stable boy to the ground, and rounded up Thomas's animals. Thomas thought he should run to the stable boy's defense, but the boy rose on his own and ran off down the road, limping and holding his injured arm. Thomas watched the soldiers tie his horses to the back of their own. His favorite old mare was nearly lame and she was blind in one eye, but they took her also.

They took his sheep and his swine in more wagons. There was nothing left but a few chickens running around the yard cackling in protest to the intrusion. Thomas prayed John was on his way. The Culpepper family needed to get out of England before one or more of them ended up on the executioner's block, if not for past actions of defending the king then for current actions of killing these soldiers for violating his home and destroying his property.

CHAPTER 27

August 1649, The Thomas and John

John received his brother's letter in June and sailed for London that very moment. His ship had been provisioned and ready to sail for months, since he received word of the king's execution.

After two long months of stormy seas, he finally anchored his ship at the mouth of the Thames. John knew he couldn't sail into London without attracting a lot of unwanted attention. He also knew the mouth of the River Medway lay at the end of the Thames, but it was too narrow and shallow for his ship to navigate. Though it was late in the evening when they arrived, the men lowered a small boat into the water, and John and Benjamin rowed into the inlet of the Medway, which would take them from the Thames all the way down to Maidstone. Leeds Castle lay three miles from the center of town.

"Do you know exactly where to find your family?" Benjamin asked as they rowed.

"My brother's letter said our wives and children are hiding in the cellar at Leeds Castle. I just hope they're still there."

"And your brother?"

"He said he'll be watching from afar. He'll come to us."

"Are we in danger here, Cap'n?"

"Most likely. If they're searching for my brother, they'll certainly detain me to locate him, so I think it best we remain hidden."

John and Benjamin rowed silently for hours, listening to the frogs croak and watching bats fly overhead. Hours after the sky had turned to black, they reached Maidstone. They tied their rowboat behind a shack that displayed a wooden sign on its rickety dock. The sign read *Waller's*. John was grateful the fisherman's shack was still there, and he hoped the man would help them. He tapped on the door and told the sleepy man his mother from the Blackwall Inn had sent them. The man scratched his head and gestured for John and Benjamin to come in. In the pale fire light, he greeted them with warm blue eyes, eyes just like John's.

The trio spent the rest of the night and the next day resting by a small fireplace, eating eel and bream, and hiding in the back rooms. The fisherman told them of the battle that had occurred at Maidstone, and John felt his palms sweat at the thought of how terrified his wife must have been, listening to the thunder of cannon and musket fire.

When the darkness of evening fell, John and Benjamin thanked Waller for his hospitality and resumed their trek to Leeds Castle. They weaved their way in the dark between shacks and cottages and came out in the clearing at the edge of town. They walked three miles down the dusty road to Leeds Castle.

When the white castle loomed before them, they stayed hidden in the bushes, watching and waiting for any movement, either from the castle or from soldiers who might have followed them. They saw none on either count. The land was still and the sky was clear, filled with bright stars and a full moon. John stared at the castle for a few minutes. He puckered his lips and began making bird sounds. Benjamin looked at him like he had lost his mind. After receiving no response from the castle's inhabitants, John emerged from the bushes and walked into the middle of the road, still making the sounds. He walked straight toward the mote, in plain sight. Benjamin looked around, half expecting soldiers to come charging toward John at any moment. When none came, Benjamin tiptoed up behind John, looking over his shoulder with each step.

Suddenly, the drawbridge creaked and slowly began to lower. John turned and looked at Benjamin with a huge grin on his face. Benjamin shook his head.

"I knew my son would wonder why a bird was singing at night and would come to investigate. Henry would recognize my silhouette instantly."

As soon as John and Benjamin crossed the bridge, it began to raise behind them. John and Benjamin remained still in the middle of the courtyard that had long ago seen better days. Weeds grew from every crevasse. The ground was covered with waste from goats and chickens. The family had obviously been locked up here for quite some time. They remained motionless and waited for the bridge to come to a stop. Once it stopped and the night air was again silent, Henry appeared from the shadows, looking so much taller and with a more manly physique than John remembered.

"Henry! I knew you'd know it was me." John held his arms out to the boy.

"Father!" Seventeen-year-old Henry ran to John and allowed himself to be enfolded in his arms. "I knew you'd come." They hugged for a long time.

"Benjamin, you remember my eldest,

Henry, who has obviously become a grown man in my long absence." John ruffled the boy's hair. "Henry, this is Benjamin, the first mate of the *Thomas and John* and the best sailor you'll ever meet."

The two shook hands.

"It's a pleasure to see you again, sir," Henry said.

"And you, my boy."

Henry nodded.

"I'm here to collect you all and take you to the ship. Where's your mother?"

"I'm right here, John," a soft voice said from the shadows.

John turned and saw his wife step into the moonlight. She was the most beautiful sight he had seen in a long, long time. He took a step toward her and they looked into each other's eyes for a moment before he wrapped her in his arms. "Mary, oh my Mary. How I've missed you. Is everyone all right?"

"Yes, we're all fine. We haven't seen Thomas for months, though. We suspect he's in hiding."

"He said in a letter to me that he's doing just that, but he will meet us at the ship."

She began to sob. "Oh, John, they've taken everything. We've been forced to hide here for so long, nearly a year."

"I know, my dear, and I suspect they will take Leeds Castle sooner or later. We need to get you all out of here."

"And go where?"

"To Virginia."

"Virginia?"

"We'll discuss it once we're all together on the ship and safe. When the children rise, tell them to pack their things. We will rest here for the day and leave at sundown."

CHAPTER 28

Leeds Castle

The family spent the day together in the cellar's secret rooms, and John was happy to be reacquainted with his boys after not seeing them for over a year. They had grown so much in his absence. Where did the time go? They discussed the coming voyage on the ship and the small village of Accomac. James and Denny, now ten and twelve, were vocal about their excitement to travel to Virginia, but Mary and Katherine were nervous about the idea. John knew Mary never wanted her sons to board a ship, but now she had no choice. She didn't say anything. She just wrung her hands and stared wide-eyed at John. He reassured her it would be a great adventure for the boys, and it would also be safe.

Robbie, who had just turned nine, said, "Father, are there Indians in Virginia?"

"Yes, there are, but we trade with them and they're friendly," John answered.

"I've never seen an Indian," Robbie said.

"No, I wouldn't think you have, but you will very soon."

"How long will it take to get there?" asked John's eighteen-year-old nephew, Alex.

"If the weather is good, it'll take about six weeks." John pulled his youngest son, six-year-old Johnny, up on his lap and bounced him up and down. "We'll ride the waves just like this. Won't that be fun?"

Johnny giggled. Mary watched him and gave a faint smile. "It's good to have you home, John." She waved her hands around the room. "Although this isn't home."

John looked at her with great love and tenderness. "Home is wherever we are together. Perhaps we will live happily in Virginia and we'll never have to separate again."

Lines of worry crossed her brow.

"You'll like Virginia, Mary. There aren't as many amenities as you're used to here, but I'm sure you'll find the land quite beautiful."

She nodded reluctantly. "I'm sure I will."

CHAPTER 29

To the Ship

As darkness fell, John and Benjamin rounded up the horses. They had not been tended for the last year and were roaming free around the castle. The men hitched the skittish horses to two old hay wagons and loaded up the women and nine children. John carried Mary and their boys. Benjamin carried Katherine and her children. Katherine's eldest, Anna, who was now twenty, sat on the front bench with Benjamin. If any soldiers crossed their path, they would simply look like a poor couple heading home for the evening. Katherine and her three other children were kept hidden under a tarp in the back, in case they ran into anyone who would recognize her and demand to know where her husband was.

John kept his distance from Benjamin as they began their three-mile trek back to Maidstone. A loon sang in the distance as the wagon wheels made a grinding noise in the dirt. A mile into their journey, they had seen nothing unusual and Mary began to relax a bit.

"John, are you sure we're doing the right thing?" she whispered.

John nodded and patted her knee in reassurance.

"How are we going to get to the ship?"

"I've made arrangements. Don't worry."

When they arrived at Maidstone, Waller had four rowboats waiting for them. They left the boat John and Benjamin rowed in on for Thomas, who would certainly follow them. The family would row up the River Medway toward the ship, with only the light from the full moon. John hoped it would be enough. Once they arrived at the ship, they would wait until dawn for Thomas. Benjamin had asked what they would do if Thomas didn't show up by dawn, but John told him that wasn't a possibility. He knew his brother. Thomas would be there.

During the last mile of their trek, John kept looking over his shoulder for signs of his brother. He never saw anything, but was quite convinced the loon he had heard went by the name of Thomas. He didn't mention the thought to anyone. Obviously Thomas had grown adept at staying hidden. The idea of the family soon being reunited brought a grin to John's face.

Though cramped and uncomfortable, the family made the journey to the River Medway unscathed. They saw no soldiers. No one crossed their path or interrupted their journey. The moon watched over them and the loon occasionally sounded from behind. When they arrived at Waller's, John and Benjamin helped the women and children into the four rowboats that awaited them, all the time thanking Waller for his assistance.

"Any friend of my mother's is a friend of mine," Waller assured them.

Benjamin made John's two eldest sons honorary sailors, putting Henry in charge of the third boat and Alex in charge of the fourth. Henry's face lit up. He and Benjamin chatted at the back of the watery caravan for hours as they paddled up the Medway toward the Thames.

"You're quite enjoying this adventure, eh, Henry?" Benjamin asked.

"Yes, sir."

"Well, wait until you ride the ocean and feel the spray on your face. The sail will grab the wind and it will feel like you're flying like a bird. You've never gone that fast before. You're in for quite a journey."

"I'm looking forward to it, sir."

"Shhh," John said from the front boat.

They all stopped paddling and drifted slowly, silently forward. John waved his hands at Benjamin and the boys, indicating for them to move their boats to the tree line and wait. Frogs protested from the edges of the green banks. Except for the slight ripples caused by the gliding oars, the water was still and flat. The air was humid and silent. The *Thomas and John* floated in the distance, looming high above the waterline, like a building in the middle of the river. Mary didn't realize the ship was so large, as she had never seen the vessel anchored. She had only seen it tied to a dock, where the bottom half was hidden from view by the pier.

Mary gasped and pointed forward. Everyone saw them at the same time. Circling the ship were four smaller boats. The hair on the back of John's neck stood up, but thankfully he and Benjamin had prepared for just such an intrusion. They had sanded the ship's name off the back of the stern. No flags of pedigree flew atop the masts. All the ship's papers had been left behind in Virginia. Anything indicating the vessel's ownership had been carefully and completely removed.

John turned to the others and whispered, "Remain close to the shore, up in the trees, where they can't see you. I'll take care of this." He paddled his boat forward, with his sons Denny and James in it.

"Denny, reach under your seat and find a

bundled cloth," John whispered.

Denny did so and placed it on his lap.

"Open it."

Denny carefully unfolded the layers and found hunting knives.

"Take one and hide it on you so you can get to it readily. I know you're not soldiers, but if this turns into a battle, you're going to have to be men and do what needs to be done. If you have to use the knife, don't be afraid to do so. If these soldiers are planning to do us any harm, we will not go down without a fight. I vow to get your mother to safety, and I expect you to do the same."

"We will do what we must, Father," James said, not the slightest quiver in his voice.

"Ahoy," John yelled to the boats as they neared the ship.

"Are you the owner of this ship, sir?" asked one of the men.

"Yes, I am. How can I help you?" John counted the boats and the men. Four boats, filled with four men each. Sixteen. His boys would be no match for these soldiers, but he knew Benjamin watched from a distance, not to mention Thomas, who was surely close behind, and every member of John's crew, who watched from decks and would fire upon these soldiers without hesitation if they thought their captain was in trouble.

He took a deep breath. These soldiers had

not yet boarded his ship, but they were obviously interested in doing so.

"We would like to know why you've left your ship here at the mouth of the river instead of bringing her into dock."

"I just arrived and heard there was a governmental shift in the country. I wanted to go into town and check if the tariffs or taxes had changed before I brought her to dock."

"And did you find that information?"

"No, I'm afraid I couldn't find anyone in charge. Perhaps you could tell me who to speak with."

"As far as we know, Parliament hasn't changed any seafaring laws, but if you want specifics, you'd have to go to the House of Commons and check with Oliver Cromwell."

"I don't have time for that sort of nonsense. I'm on a strict schedule."

"Who are those men with you?" the man asked.

"These are not men, they're mere boys. Just my sailors. I thought I'd leave them on the dock to help bring her in if I could get some information. Alas, I guess we'll be on our way to the next port."

"Boys! What are your names?"

"Will Meyer and my brother Ben, sir," Denny yelled without hesitation.

"Very well, then. We are watching for any traitors who may try to escape. Don't take anyone on board with you, no matter what story they give you. You could be held on charges of abetting a criminal."

"You don't need to worry about this ship. We only transport goods, but thank you for the warning."

"Very well. Good evening…um, what did you say your name was?"

"I didn't, but if you'd like to sit out here in the cold and dark and discuss it further, I'm afraid I'm going to have to deny that request. I have to get back to work and get this ship to Denmark."

CHAPTER 30

To Virginia

The soldiers began paddling away. John and the boys watched them in silence. Once they were out of sight, John motioned to Benjamin and they got the family on board. Mary looked as if she were going to faint, her alabaster skin even paler in the moonlight.

John wrapped his arms around her. "It's almost over."

She didn't respond but allowed herself to relax in his arms. After some time, she asked, "What now? How do we find Thomas?"

"We won't find him. He'll find us."

She looked at him with great concern but didn't ask any further questions.

The boys ran around the ship, inspecting the various masts and jibs. Being out of the castle for the first time in a year, combined with their nervousness from getting to the ship, had them all nearly jumping out of their skin.

After a few hours, their mothers finally got them settled down and sleeping in the hammocks below deck. Mary stayed below with them, but Katherine didn't want to leave the deck until her husband arrived. The sailors had all gone to sleep.

The ship became quiet, almost ominous, and the moon began to set in the western sky. With every second, John and Katherine became more and more anxious. Anxious that the soldiers would return. Anxious that Thomas wouldn't show. John remained on the bow, watching for any sign of his brother. Katherine stood not far away, staring over the railing.

"What if he doesn't make it?" Benjamin whispered so Katherine couldn't hear him.

"He'll make it. Be ready to sail at first light." John's tone was assured, but his chest was tight and his stomach was turning flips. What if Thomas *didn't* make it? Should he wait longer? He couldn't leave his ship here in the river. He would have to send his family ahead with Benjamin and go back to land alone to find his brother. Where would he even begin to search? His palms were sweating, even in the coolness of the night. The ropes holding the anchors creaked against the wood. The wavelets gently splashed on the hull. John thought he could hear his own heart beating.

Benjamin walked to the foremost bow and peered into the night. He placed his hands on the railing and crossed his fingers.

Katherine clenched a handkerchief to her lips. Her eyes were like saucers as she scanned the horizon.

As the slightest lines of pink and purple lit the sky, Benjamin approached his captain. "Cap'n, should we prepare to make sail?"

John hesitated, but then he heard a loon singing faintly from the starboard side. He walked toward it with a grin. He kicked a rope ladder over the railing and said, "Yes, Benjamin, prepare to make sail." The ladder splashed into the water and within moments, a worn and very bearded Thomas popped his head above the railing.

"It's about time," John said as he helped his brother over the side.

"Me? I've been waiting for you for months."

They hugged and patted each other on the back as Katherine ran to her husband, tears in her eyes. Thomas and Katherine held each other for a long time as John pulled up the ladder and Benjamin walked around the ship, waking up his sailors. In a flurry of activity, they began pulling up anchors and climbing the masts.

When Thomas and Katherine finally let go of each other, John slapped him on the back. "Well, brother," John said, "welcome aboard the *Thomas and John*. I'm glad you finally decided to join me on a journey."

"I'm glad we bought the ship. Is everyone aboard?"

"We're all here," Katherine said.

"We were just waiting for you. Now let's get underway before Parliament decides to seize our ship." John turned to Benjamin, who stood behind him smiling a toothless grin. "Benjamin, pull up that rowboat and let's get out of here."

"Aye, Cap'n," Benjamin said, then barked orders at the crew.

The day at sea was filled with smiles, laughter, and many questions about the impending journey. By the time evening fell, the *Thomas and John* had crept its way past Margate, heading south toward Dover. She sailed through the darkness, and when daybreak began to light the sky, she entered the wide English Channel, heading west toward the ocean.

John, Thomas, and Henry stood on the bow in the dawn's light as the ship's sails caught a great wind. She bounded over the waves, riding the great swells, spray blasting her bow. Henry looked up at the sails and grinned, licking his lips to taste the salt from the spray. He grinned at his father.

John wrapped his arm around his son's shoulder and looked at his brother. "To Virginia?" he asked.

"To Virginia," they said in unison.

John yelled up to Benjamin in the crow's nest. "Take us home, Benjamin. Take us home."

"Aye, Cap'n. Home it is!" Benjamin shouted back.

THE END

Author's Notes

This book stems from decades of genealogical research by me and others. I found that in the late 1500s, there were more than a dozen Culpepper barons and earls living in England. They had enormous wealth, vast land holdings, and great manor houses, many of which are still standing today. This was the privilege John Culpepper was born into. I wondered how and why, when they possessed such great power and prestige, they chose to sail across the ocean, move to an inhospitable land, and face possible starvation and death. Why would they leave the comfort of their manors and servants to live in probable squalor and battle savage Indians? How did they end up becoming the modest people I knew in my youth in Mississippi?

As I researched the family to find which one came to America first, I ran into the problem most Culpepper researchers run into. Each man named John had a brother named Thomas. Each John and Thomas had sons named John and Thomas. As the family grew, cousins and second cousins were all named John and Thomas, and they occasionally married within the family, creating a whole new tangled web of Culpepper history. The records blurred. The history became confusing. English records were destroyed. Colonial records were incomplete. After committing the known timelines of all of the different Johns and Thomases to paper, I believe I have sorted out which one was which. In an attempt to keep them straight in the reader's mind, I have given some of them nicknames, yet they are all listed in historical records as John or Thomas. Of course, as new documents are uncovered, it is possible that my theory is just as mistaken as theories that have come before.

John Culpepper the Merchant was the first in the family to migrate to America, and as I began unraveling English and colonial history, I found the answers to the above questions of how and why they ended up in America, along with shocking tales of what happened to them once they arrived and what happened to the ones left behind. This four-book series begins on the day John was born and ends at the end of his life, but John's is not the only story here. There are far too many religious and political events and bold and brave personalities surrounding the family to ignore. These events and people shaped the man we know as John Culpepper. This series uncovers a life of passion, heroism and bravery, love and forgiveness, and ultimately truth. Truth of our history and truth about life itself.

John Culpepper is believed to be the progenitor of all American Culpeppers. He was my tenth great-grandfather.

My deepest thanks go out to those who made this book possible:

> Elyse Dinh-McCrillis — TheEditNinja.com
> Robert Hess — book designer

Warren Culpepper and Lew Griffin, who maintain the Culpepper Connections website, and all of the Culpepper descendants who contribute to it.

References

www.Culpepper Connections.com

Culpeppers of England and America
by Warren H. (Dick) Culpepper

Journal of the House of Commons: Volume 2, 1640-1643
www.British-History.ac.uk

Books by Lori Crane

Okatibbee Creek Series
Okatibbee Creek
An Orphan's Heart
Elly Hays

Stuckey's Bridge Trilogy
The Legend of Stuckey's Bridge
Stuckey's Legacy: The Legend Continues
Stuckey's Gold: The Curse of Lake Juzan

Culpepper Saga
I, John Culpepper
John Culpepper the Merchant
John Culpepper, Esquire
Culpepper's Rebellion

Other Titles
Savannah's Bluebird
Witch Dance
The Culpepper-Fairfax Scandal
On This Day: A Perpetual Calendar for Family Genealogy

About the Author

Bestselling and award-winning author Lori Crane is a writer of southern historical fiction and the occasional thriller. Her books have climbed to the Kindle Top 100 lists many times, with *Elly Hays* debuting on Amazon at #1 in Native American stories. She has also enjoyed a place among her peers in the Top 100 historical fiction authors on Amazon, climbing to #23. She is a native Mississippi belle currently residing in greater Nashville.

She is a member of the Daughters of the American Revolution, the United States Daughters of 1812, the United Daughters of the Confederacy, and the Historical Novel Society. She is also a professional musician and member of the Screen Actors Guild-American Federation of Television and Radio Artists.

Visit Lori's website at
www.LoriCrane.com

Sign up for Lori's quarterly newsletter at
http://eepurl.com/GHJ7D

An excerpt from

John Culpepper, Esquire

The third book in the Culpepper Saga

CHAPTER 1

1650, Accomac, Virginia Colony

"Sir Edmund," the servant called across the busy tavern.

Edmund Plowden was sitting alone at a table in the back of the Tan House. He looked up and saw his stable hand standing in the doorway. "Over here, boy. What is it?"

The boy approached the table. "Sir Edmund, you told me to tell you when John Culpepper returned to Accomac. His ship docked early this morning, sir."

"Very well. Thank you for letting me know." Plowden took a drink of ale.

"He's got a ship full of people with him, sir."

"What kind of people? Settlers?"

"No, sir. I heard him refer to one of the men as brother and another as son."

Plowden slammed his mug down. "That's just what this colony needs—more bloody Culpeppers." He spit tobacco on the floor and wiped his mouth on the sleeve of his shirt.

The outburst caused the room to quiet. Plowden and Culpepper had been enemies for nearly two decades. No one talked much about it, as no one liked Plowden, but everyone knew. Plowden had been jailed in England for physical abuse of his pregnant wife, but he escaped while on his way to court and ended up in Virginia. He fled England to avoid prosecution and paying alimony and any additional expenses, but since he had been in the colony, he had spent more time in court than out of it. He was involved in more than forty court cases in Virginia, but none was bad enough to land him in jail. He was simply an offensive man with a violent temper and sour disposition. Most people called him a bully, but never to his face. The only reason everyone knew about his past in England was because John Culpepper was the lawyer who had represented Mabel Plowden, Edmund's wife, and Culpepper had made no secret of what an unfortunate example of a man Plowden was.

John Culpepper, on the other hand, was a pillar of the community. He ran a merchant vessel between England and Virginia, delivering much needed wares to residents of the colony and contributing to their income by selling their produce in England. He assisted his friends and neighbors with their legal matters. He was a gracious man in his mid-forties, a distinguished member of the gentry who had always held British properness and manners in high esteem. Other men admired him, and the women thought he was probably one of the most attractive gentlemen to ever grace the shores of the Chesapeake. His prowess as a sailor had not gone unnoticed by the female persuasion. His tanned face, graced by dark curls and piercing blue eyes, was the subject of many daydreams.

Those who overheard the conversation between Plowden and his servant were glad John was back and anxious for any news about the state of England. King Charles had been tried on charges of treason and the high commissioners found him guilty as charged. In an act unprecedented in the history of England, the king was beheaded on the Tower Green on January 30, 1649. The colony had received word that the king was dead and Oliver Cromwell was now running the country, declaring the land the English Commonwealth, but the settlers had heard nothing more. They didn't know where the king's heir was. They didn't know if their families in the homeland were safe. They didn't know much of anything, as it took months for word to travel between the continents.

A few gentlemen in the inn hastily rose and left to go speak with John. Others waited for word to filter to them through other means. With a wave of his hand, Plowden rudely dismissed his servant and ordered himself another ale.

Made in the USA
San Bernardino, CA
22 July 2020